THREE GIFTS FOR CHRISTMAS

A CHRISTMAS NOVEL

BY JOHN SHIVERS

fairDALE
publications
Calhoun, GA

Printed in the United States of America

ISBN: 978-1723319235

Dedication

This story is reality because one of my persistent readers did all but demand that I write such a book. A Christmas book, specifically, he said. I've learned to listen to what my readers want, so here, Gary Thompson, is **Three Gifts for Christmas**. To repay him for his dogged determination that I could and should produce just such a work, I've named a character for him, and dedicate this book to him.

And to Elizabeth, my wife and partner in this writing life.
I love you!

Other Books by John Shivers

Create My Soul Anew Trilogy

Hear My Cry
Paths of Judgment
Lift Up Mine Eyes

◊

Renew A Right Spirit Series

Broken Spirit
Merry Heart
His Mercy Endureth
Let Not Your Hearts Be Troubled

◊

Slop Bucket Mystery Series

Boat Load of Trouble
Out of Thin Heir

◊

Repossessed

◊

Gone Astray

◊

Colorblind

Author's Note

Many times I'll get feedback from readers who tell me how much they enjoyed one of my books, and add their opinion that the book "deserves" to be a movie. Unfortunately, I have very little clout in Hollywood, Georgia and absolutely no clout whatsoever in Hollywood, California. So far, none of my books have found their way onto the big screen. Nor on the little screen, either.

If I could hope that one of my books might attract attention in "Tinsel Town," **Three Gifts for Christmas** would be that book. For probably as long as the Hallmark Movie Channel has been on the air, Elizabeth and I have enjoyed watching their offerings, most especially around the Christmas season. I will be so bold as to say that when the gist of this book was born, I actually saw it as and compared it to a Hallmark movie. Several people who have read the first draft of the story have agreed.

This is the first time I've written a Christmas-themed book, but I must admit that I truly enjoyed it. So much so, that I may consider doing it again for Christmas 2019. You'll just have to check back and see!

In the meantime… Hallmark! Are you listening?

Christmas 2018

Think about it…

When you buy a book from an author
you're buying more than a story.

You are buying numerous hours of errors and rewrites.

You are buying moments of frustration and
moments of sheer joy.

You are not buying just a book, you are buying something
they delight in sharing;

a piece of their heart, a piece of their soul…
a small piece of someone's life.

CHAPTER ONE

A Cold New Beginning

I t should have been a great morning walk.

The air was infused with a crispness that summoned forth memories of earlier, wonderful times of cold weather play and family fun. The last of the season's palette of color still adorned the many trees that surrounded the small, secluded enclave of Cedar Mountain, Georgia. Rebekka Austin knew walking should have been an enjoyable exercise. And it would have been, had the need to bundle up and hoof it several blocks in near pre-dawn darkness been a voluntary action.

When said walk was by necessity, because no other options existed, the enjoyment factor was greatly diminished.

"I'm cold, Mommie. How far now?"

"Just a couple of more blocks, sweetie." Rebekka consciously slowed her stride, even though she risked being late for her own job. Again. Aimee was almost four years old. To her, an eight block walk through nippy temperatures must be a gargantuan task. Just the latest of too many tasks, Rebekka had to admit, this precious child had been subjected to over the past few months.

When your innocent child protested the exertion, for certain all the fun had been leeched from what otherwise might have been an exciting adventure.

"Look, Aimee," she encouraged. "Look up ahead. See? There's the church."

"Yes, Mommie. I see it. But I can't walk that far."

Rebekka shifted her tote strap to the other shoulder and stooped to her daughter's level. "Here, sweetie, let me carry you. Then you know you can get there."

"Uh-uh; too big to be carried."

Her daughter was indeed a heavy load. At the same time, if it meant Aimee got to the pre-school program at the First Community Church, and she could get to her teaching job at the high school and not have to explain another tardiness to the principal, it was worth the strain on her back. She would recover. She hoped.

She scooped the child into her arms and, despite protests to the contrary, began to make deliberate strides towards the side door into the educational wing of the church building, where she and her daughter had finally begun attending worship. Their presence, she realized, was both reluctant and sometimes spasmodic, but it was what it was.

Aimee had been safely handed off to Patti Martin, the lead teacher, and Rebekka consulted her watch as she left the building. Two blocks to go, and four minutes before late-sign-in. With any luck, she might make it just under the wire. If she didn't, she reminded herself, this setback would be only the latest in a series of devastating incidents that had begun in the wee hours of the morning only eight months before.

If only she could have known then what she knew now?

* * * * *

The ringing of the phone had dragged a grumbling, bleary-eyed Rebekka Austin from her restful sleep. "Darryl," she called out to her husband, as she punched his side of the bed, seeking to awaken him. "Phone's ringing." For starters, the phone was on his side of the bed, and besides, no call at… she squinted at the clock across the room… at three-thirty-seven in the morning could be anything but bad news. Better that Darryl handle it. He was a cop; bad news was one of the things he dealt with. Then she remembered. Her husband wasn't in bed. He was working the overnight shift because of a manpower shortage. Desperate to catch it before the caller hung up, she dived across the bed to grab the offending noisemaker.

"Hello?"

"Mrs. Austin?"

The man's voice was vaguely familiar. "Who is this?"

"This is Captain Hunsaker."

Darryl's captain. This can't be good.

"Yes?" she answered cautiously.

"I'm outside your front door. Can you come and let me in?"

A frigid wave of dread washed over her at that moment, and if she were truthful, full body warmth had yet to be totally restored, even months later. She still had no memory of getting to the front door, or of opening it to discover the Captain, along with Chuck Boston, Darryl's partner and close friend. Behind them, she had glimpsed Dr. Ted Watson, the pastor of their church.

She had slight recall of the floor coming up to meet her. Her next memory, which she had finally understood was two days after the funeral, had been of Judith Austin. Darryl's mother. Standing in the middle of Rebekka's living room, she had decreed that Rebekka was responsible for her son's death. "If God had approved of your union," the tall woman under the platinum blonde beehive had declared, "He wouldn't have taken my son from me!"

Never mind He also took my husband from me and robbed Aimee of her daddy. But Rebekka said nothing to refute her mother-in-law's words. Rebuttal would have been no more effective this time, than it had been any of the many other times, when the two had butted heads in the five years she and Darryl were married.

She didn't like me as Darryl's wife, so she's sure not going to like me as his widow! Rebekka could accept the woman's dislike for her. It was nothing new. What hurt to the quick was the woman's total dismissal of the only grandchild she would ever have. In this grandmother's eyes, at least, her son's precious daughter still didn't exist.

That encounter with her mother-in-law might have been the latest skirmish in an ongoing battle, but it was far from the last confrontation between the two women. Even when Rebekka worked to avoid the conflict, to keep whatever tenuous peace might exist between them, it was almost like Darryl's mother went out of her way to engage. To engage and wound, whenever possible.

Rebekka had been left a widow because her husband sacrificed his life to defend and rescue another woman. A wife whose husband had been intent on killing her. It had been a most bitter pill to swallow. But swallowing was nothing compared to the burden of living with the truth day after day. When the car needed new tires, Darryl hadn't been there to deal with matters. It wasn't that Rebekka couldn't do it, but she would always wonder if she'd been seen as an easy target?

Just paying the ongoing monthly bills had suddenly become an overwhelming task, and without Darryl's paycheck going into their bank account twice a month, what little cushion was there had quickly evaporated like the heavy dews on an early June morning. She had stretched the money as far as she could, but still the total steadily dwindled. She and Darryl had made the decision to live close to the bone, so that she might stay home with Aimee. On those few occasions when she saw others spend so freely, and without worry, she had found herself envious and a little angry. But a simple glance at her daughter, who was already reading simple sentences, convinced her that she had the best world.

It wasn't lost on her, however, that Darryl had accepted the additional shift because of the money. Except for that, they might still be an intact family.

"Had the best world…" were the right words at the time. After Darryl was gone, she found herself questioning their judgment. There were days when the grocery list contained more items than she could afford, and she found herself marking off all unnecessary wishes, and buying store-brand products instead of name brand. More than once, Aimee had begged for her favorite snacks that simply hadn't been in the budget.

Perhaps the two most cruel realizations had been over her husband's life insurance, and the cost of his burial. Sticker shock at what even a modest funeral would run, had brought Rebekka to near hysterics. Yet his mother had been right there, demanding that her son not be "put away on the cheap." While she knew she couldn't afford the final total, Rebekka understood that her husband's life insurance proceeds would help pay the bill. Desperate for peace, she had caved to Judith Austin's demands.

Rebekka had never been sure if the funeral director was looking out for her, or himself, but when he queried Judith on how much she planned to contribute to the cost of the funeral, her mother-in-law had declared, "Not one thin dime. I didn't kill my son."

Like I did kill him? The new widow felt like she had been sucker-punched.

The rug was pulled out from under her a second time, when she learned minutes before the service, that there would be no life insurance proceeds. Nothing to pay for the funeral, nothing to replace her husband's paycheck. Re-establishing herself was, at that moment, the farthest thing from Rebekka's mind. But it didn't matter. There was no money to fund any kind of a future.

Darryl was killed three weeks before his life insurance would have gone into force. Three weeks!!

Rebekka wasn't certain whether her lack of recall of the service had been due to the shock of his death, or the realization that she was burying the love of her life and had no way to pay for that burial. Before they left the cemetery, Captain Hunsaker and Chuck Boston had fallen into step beside her, and quietly shared that members of the force would pool their resources to help offset the funeral costs. She still wasn't certain if she had ever thanked them.

There were many who had been there for her in the beginning. But that number dwindled as the weeks flipped past. Now she could literally count those people who extended her little if any sympathy. For one thing, her situation had managed to split the church family that initially had been so supportive. Thanks to Judith, who seemed determined to drive a wedge and force church members to choose sides, Rebekka had watched herself become a virtual pariah.

* * * * *

"You barely made it again this morning. Sign in by seven-thirty. No exceptions."

Rebekka was bent over the keyboard logging in for the day, when the principal's voice laid waste to all the positive thoughts she'd cultivated as she ran for the main office at Cedar Mountain High School. Her drama class was set to select the play they would present in the spring, and she was already evaluating casting possibilities.

"Yes sir," I'm here. She stole a glance at the screen, assuring herself that it had logged her in at seven twenty-nine. Anything past seven-thirty would have been tardy, and she would have had to beg the principal to allow her to teach her classes that day. Computer sign-in denied anyone the chance to fudge, and Principal Hawkins was a micromanaging stickler for punctuality.

"You know," the administrator said, "you just need to leave home earlier."

"Yes, sir," was her response, although Rebekka wanted so badly to ask him if he had any idea what it was like to propel a toddler each morning and deal with no car as well. But she held her tongue. Some people in town were already too aware of her plight, and she didn't intend to give this man any further ammunition to use against her. She couldn't share that her car wasn't running, or that the repair estimate was greater than she could cover, until she had time to save some money.

Until then, Aimee and I will be walking. She resolved to get

18

her daughter into bed earlier in the evening, and wake her at least fifteen minutes earlier each morning. That should handle the time problem, but it did nothing to address the colder weather that was rapidly becoming more severe.

The day went quickly. Rebekka taught her English and American Literature classes, and the drama class had selected its play for the spring production. Auditions began that day. The enjoyment her job gave her was the main factor that brought Rebekka to work each morning. That, and the check she drew at the end of the month.

They had emptied the milk jug that morning at breakfast, and Rebekka elected to swing through The Green Spot grocery store before she picked up Aimee. Shopping was so much simpler, especially when money was tight, when Aimee wasn't along to find something on each aisle that she simply had to have. The detour through the supermarket didn't take long. While there were plenty of empty spots in her pantry and refrigerator, filling those spots would have to wait until payday that was still three days away.

Three days. Right at that moment, as she counted out change from her pocket to pay for the gallon of milk that couldn't wait, the time felt more like three months. Getting accustomed to a monthly payday, when there was no cushion to soften the blow and the month lasted longer than the money, had been rough. Still, she was thankful for the check that magically resuscitated her bank account the last day of every month. But every payday was gone before she could turn around, it seemed. Aimee drew a Social Security check from Darryl, but even with it, there never was any wiggle room.

Rebekka wondered as she stood in the checkout line, with the heavy jug of milk hugged up against her, if the rest of her life would be like the last few months. Just the possibility that things might be as good as they were ever going to get made her want to drop the milk and bolt, to escape from the store, Cedar Mountain, and from the nightmare of the past few months.

But she couldn't do that to Aimee. That poor child had already seen one parent snatched from her, Rebekka lectured herself. To deprive her daughter of the other parent would be beyond cruel. Instead, she parted with the pocket change, took her milk and had soon walked to the church to reclaim her child. One of the immediate charms of the small mountain town, she'd noticed, was that it was an easy walk all over town. Once she'd exchanged notes with Patti, and received her assignment for brownies for the class party on Friday, she and Aimee set out for home.

Home. What a wonderful image the word conveyed. Unfortunately, Rebekka reflected, the reality of the small, furnished, single-wide rental trailer she'd managed to snag for housing, didn't quite live up to the grandeur befitting the word home. Still and all, she'd been grateful to get the little mobile home. In Atlanta, they'd lived in a rental apartment. Darryl had always promised them a house as soon as Aimee was in school, and Rebekka could go back to work. She was back at work, but the prospect of a house had been blasted to smithereens at the same time the enraged, abusive husband had blown away the love of her life.

The prospect of always living in the little two-bedroom cottage on wheels was suddenly so distasteful and overpowering, Rebekka had to lecture herself to count her blessings. Sometimes it wasn't so easy to do.

Supper was a chicken and potato casserole she'd put together the previous evening. After she slid it into the hot oven, she pulled together a basic green salad, baked some brown and serve rolls, and she and Aimee were soon enjoying their meal.

"What did you do at school today?" she asked. "Who's having the birthday party on Friday?"

The custom at the pre-school was to host one party each month for all the children celebrating birthdays in that month.

"Reisa and Toby," Aimee said, around a mouthful of salad. Rebekka offered silent thanks yet again that her daughter enjoyed vegetables. So many children, she knew, had to be cajoled or even forced to eat anything green. "When do I get to have my birthday?" Aimee asked.

"What month is your birthday?"

Aimee laid down her fork, put her elbow on the table and cupped her chin in her hand. Rebekka literally saw the light bulb in her daughter's head begin to glow.

"Febunary."

"Feb-ru-ary," she corrected. "That's right, you were born in February. So what month is this?"

"Oc... Ocober...."

Her child was getting flustered. "October. You almost had it. This is October."

"October. So how long?" She child's face lit up. "Saturday is Halloween."

"That's right, it is. So next month is November, then December. Then January and February. So how many months is that?"

Aimee appeared to be calculating and finally began to count on her fingers. Math had been Darryl's favorite subject in school, and almost before his daughter had been able to speak, he'd been teaching her to count. As a result, the little girl had entered preschool far advanced in math, even though her socialization skills had been lacking.

When they'd first arrived in town, Aimee had been enrolled in a private day care that had closed abruptly due to the owner's sudden illness. The only other option had been the church-run day care, the one place she'd hesitated to place her. Rebekka had endured enough of religion, but judging by how happy her daughter was, she had to conclude it had been the best move.

"Four!" Aimee crowed, interrupting her mother's trip down memory lane. "In four months I'll have my birthday at school."

"And how old will you be?"

"Four!" the child had squealed with delight. "I be four years old."

"That's right," Rebekka said, lavishing praise on the little girl who meant the world to her. After all, the child with the spun silk blond hair and captivating blue eyes was her last link with the husband who had swept her off her feet the first night they met.

How she could have been so deliriously over the moon then, and so deep in muddy despair just now, was still more than her mind could process. How could it all have gone sour so quickly? Literally in the blink of an eye.

After they finished eating, Rebekka made quick work of tidying the kitchen. Then true to her vow earlier in the day, she changed into her gown, and convinced Aimee to get into her pajamas. They simply had to get out of the house earlier each morning. Tomorrow morning, she promised herself, would be the first day of making that happen.

She still had papers to grade and lesson plans to review, but her first responsibility was to get the little girl who was still wound up from an exciting day into bed and off to sleep. The easiest way to get to Aimee was to read to her, and the two soon settled down. For the next thirty minutes, they reread some of her daughter's favorite books. Then Rebekka introduced a new book she'd checked out from the public library. It was above Aimee's reading capability, but not her comprehension level, and it was that new and unexpected content that finally lulled the little girl off to sleep.

Rebekka carefully eased out of bed, tucked the child's covers, kissed her lightly, and left the room. With any luck, her daughter would sleep until morning. Rebekka, meanwhile, had several tasks waiting before she could escape to her own bed. Seating herself at the breakfast table, she pulled student papers from her tote and began to mark them. She missed the big desk she'd had in the apartment in Atlanta, but the trailer had been fully furnished, and wasn't large enough to accommodate the desk. Most of their possessions were in storage in Atlanta, and she paid the monthly bill religiously, even if it meant skimping on food for herself.

Darryl had loved the shows on TV where people bid on abandoned storage units and bought the contents. She was determined that what little she and Aimee had would never go that way, and was almost obsessed with being sure the rental was paid before the due date. That wasn't easy some months. And very often, Aimee lamented the loss of something that had been in her room.

For Rebekka, it wasn't the absence of material possessions that cut so sharply, as it was the abandonment of her lifelong dream. Since she'd been a young teen, she'd dreamed of someday being a writer. The vision was so real she could literally close her eyes and see it happening. Darryl had been totally supportive, so while she hadn't held down a paying job outside the home, she had devoted some time each day to speculative writing. Her reward had been the publication of several articles and, on more than one occasion, a small check besides. She couldn't have treasured those slips of paper that represented money any more, if they'd been made for millions of dollars.

Since she'd lost Darryl, she'd also lost the time as well as the inspiration to write. Between struggling to pay the bills, caring for Aimee, who had been very clingy in the beginning, fighting her mother-in-law, and trying to find a path on which to go forward, there had been no opportunity to write. Since landing in Cedar Mountain, between the loss of her office and files, her exhaustion factor – teaching high school students was hard – and the emotional toll the relocation had extracted, she simply hadn't allowed it to happen. Too, there was just something so uninspiring about working at the kitchen table, where multi-purpose was the name of the game. What she wouldn't give to have her own desk again.

When she finally finished with the papers, she reviewed the lesson plans for the remainder of the week. Tomorrow was Wednesday. How she wished it were Friday, although she remembered her mother cautioning against wishing her life away. How ironic, she thought, Mama and Daddy were both gone. So had it done her mother any good to caution against wanting the calendar to move faster?

For a long time, she'd almost forgotten the loss of her parents. But since Darryl had been killed, her parents were on her mind almost constantly. She had found herself almost angry that Darryl had gone on to be with them, while she'd been left behind. It wasn't logical, she knew. But it didn't stop her from being bummed out when she allowed her personal pity party to crank up to full force.

Her father, whom she'd adored, had been killed in an accident several hours from home, on the construction site where he was supervising a crew digging underground tunnels. She could still remember the afternoon the call came. She and Darryl had been married only a few months, and it had been all she could do to summon him from his patrol, before she'd totally lost it.

Then came what appeared at the time to be the hardest part. They went together to break the news to her mother, who had appeared to handle the death of her husband with courage and resolve. Indeed, her mother had taken charge of the arrangements, while Rebekka had been reduced to a sobbing mess of emotions. But the worst had been yet to come. Within hours after the funeral she'd thought would never end, she'd been summoned. Her mother was in the ER and she needed to come. Quick.

Two hours later, her mother was gone, too. Heart attack was

the official verdict. More likely, the doctor had confided in Darryl, a broken heart. Rebekka had been stunned to learn that there really was such a thing as a broken heart, and that it could prove fatal. From that point on, when the guilt feelings would show themselves, she'd questioned if she could have done more to help her mother adjust to her newly-widowed status. Had she deserted her parent when her mother needed her most?

Only after she experienced widowhood herself did she decide there was nothing else she could have done. Instead, she herself felt like leaving to join Darryl, were it not for Aimee. Still, she couldn't totally banish the occasional feeling that she was literally an orphan. As an only child, she'd never had siblings. Both parents and now Darryl were gone. Aimee was all she had.

It was apt to be that way for a long time. Maybe forever.

She quickly laid out breakfast preparations, turned out the lights, said goodbye to her latest visit to a past she couldn't change, and headed for bed. She set the clock for fifteen minutes earlier, and soon settled down. It was good to acknowledge what you did have, instead of dwelling on what you'd lost, what you didn't have, and what you probably wouldn't ever have.

Her efforts to get to work on time the next morning appeared to be working. She got up when the alarm sounded, Aimee was cooperative, breakfast went quickly, and they were actually out the door and on their way a good twenty minutes early. Rebekka silently congratulated herself. Aimee was animated and excited to get to school. Which was why her exuberance translated into ripped pants when she jumped a small wall within sight of the church.

Rebekka quickly examined the damage and realized the pants were too badly torn for her daughter to wear throughout the day. Nothing to do but turn around, go back home and change pants. She glanced at her watch. Up until now, they had been ahead of the game.

"Come on, Aimee," she said, as she grabbed her daughter's hand. "We're going to have to run."

While it only took about five minutes to reach the trailer, to Rebekka their mad dash felt hours long. They quickly exchanged the torn pants for another pair. They didn't coordinate with the shirt Aimee wore, Rebekka acknowledged, but there wasn't time to correct that issue as well. Then they were on their way back to pre-school, where Rebekka checked her in at the usual time. And when she logged in at school a few minutes later, she was relieved to see that once again, she'd slid in at seven-twenty-nine.

"You need to get here earlier," the principal had said from his post across the office. "You need time to collect your thoughts before you began working with your students."

"Yes, sir," she said. There was much more she could have said, but Rebekka suddenly felt too weary to even fight for herself. She was doing the very best she could do. If that wasn't good enough, then it simply wasn't good enough.

CHAPTER TWO

How Do You Pay What You Don't Have?

T he remainder of the week literally flew by in one respect, and absolutely dragged at the same time. Rebekka and Aimee ate family night supper at the church that Wednesday night. The motivation was more of a financial and convenience factor and less about the fellowship enjoyed around the table. For only $3.00, she could feed the both of them a good, hot meal, one she didn't have to go home and prepare and clean up after. Some people took home additional meals from the food that was always left over, but Rebekka hadn't yet allowed herself to look that needy.

Before Darryl's death, the three of them had been consistent in their attendance and worship in their church in Atlanta. The midweek church supper had always been on the calendar, and Darryl had often been able to arrange his schedule to join them for the meal. After his death, after her mother-in-law had launched her accusations against her, Rebekka had seen the demeanor of the church change. Over time, that change had developed into a true separation of spirit. After all, Judith gave liberally to her church, but she also never allowed the church to forget her generosity.

Rebekka and Aimee had been on the outside and before long, had stopped attending church anywhere. Only after their move to Cedar Mountain had they begun going again, and only then because Rebekka felt shamed because she didn't worship somewhere on Sunday mornings.

Thursday and Friday mornings had gone somewhat better timewise. She had actually made it to school fifteen minutes before deadline on Friday. Although her principal had witnessed her signing in well before seven-thirty, he'd offered no words of congratulations or encouragement. Rebekka forced herself to consider the temperament of the man who was her boss, and just whispered silent thanks that she'd actually managed to get them both to their respective places with time to spare. She was proud of herself, even if no one else would acknowledge her accomplishment.

Unfortunately, the day wouldn't end as positively as it began. During her lunch break, she'd scooted home to grab a book she decided she could use to illustrate a point she would be making in her afternoon American lit class. A quick check of the mailbox at the end of the driveway revealed that her carrier, like her, had been a little ahead of schedule. The box held several pieces of first class mail, as well as the usual junk that always went straight to recycle.

As she quickly thumbed through the various white envelopes, she spied one from Whitwell Mortuary and Crematory.

That's the funeral home that handled Darryl's service.

Expecting it to be a note of appreciation for her business, Rebekka was stunned to read the short letter inside. While its tone was cordial, the unsaid was terribly menacing and blunt. She thought she would never be able to forget the one sentence that was the thrust of the message.

There remains an outstanding balance on your husband's burial of $1,431.22, which is due in our office within ten days of the date of this letter.

They had spouted other platitudes, of course, but in her sinking heart, Rebekka understood. According to the date at the top of the letter, she was expected to pay money she didn't have by that same time the next week. They didn't give her any wiggle room. Nor, she thought, did they exhibit much concern.

She was so bummed out, Rebekka didn't even bother going into the house for the book she needed. Instead, she stuffed the mail into her tote, and made her way back to school. The remainder of the afternoon dragged by, and when she finally signed out that afternoon, all she could think about was how she might find the money to repair the car and pay off Darryl's funeral over the course of the next week. The task appeared impossible, and she consoled herself with the belief that things could only get better from there.

On the way home, since her payroll check should be in the

account by that point, she detoured by the bank to withdraw the money for November's rent. Her landlord required cash, and since the bank would be closed on Saturday and the first day of November was on Sunday, she elected to get the money in hand before going to claim Aimee from pre-school.

"Hey, Rebekka," Patti Martin called out as Rebekka crossed the lobby area headed to Aimee's room. "The kiddos are in here watching a movie." She pointed to a doorway nearby,

"Sorry I'm late," Rebekka said. "Had to zip through the bank."

"Not a problem," the pre-school teacher assured her. "After all those sweets at the party, this was the easiest way to occupy them."

Rebekka smiled. If they were watching a movie, then Aimee probably hadn't even realized that her mother was running late. She remembered the first week or so, her little girl had gone into meltdown mode if Rebekka hadn't shown up exactly when all the other students left.

"Say," Patti asked, "what's Aimee doing for Halloween?"

Rebekka had to admit she hadn't given a lot of thought to the next evening. This would be the first year that her daughter would want to trick-or-treat, and it would seem cruel to deny her that opportunity. Plus, if she stayed home, she'd have to buy treats for all the children who would arrive at her door. That thought sobered her.

"Bad mother that I am," she confessed, "I hadn't thought that far ahead."

"So why don't you and Aimee come to our house tomorrow night. We'll eat and then we can take both kids out together." She flashed an especially engaging smile at Rebekka. "Besides, you're new in town. You don't even know the neighborhoods."

Patti's daughter, Merry Beth, was only two months older than Aimee, and she knew her daughter would enjoy the companionship. Silently, she told herself, she would enjoy the adult companionship, especially in a town where she still knew only the main thoroughfares. The invitation was gratefully accepted, Aimee collected, and the two were soon on their walk home.

"So did you have fun at the party today?"

Her daughter's initial answer was a beaming, toothy smile. "Uh-huh, Mommie. It was a lot of fun. But what am I going to be for Halloween?" She tucked her lower lip between her teeth. "Everybody at school was talking about what they were going to be, and I didn't know what to say."

Rebekka immediately felt the guilt roll over her, even though she'd been mulling that same question, wondering just how much she would have to spend to create a costume for Aimee that wouldn't embarrass her daughter. In truth, however, the guilt was deserved. She should have been on top of everything long before now.

"So what would you like to be?"

Almost as if she couldn't walk and talk, Aimee halted, twirled around, and with another toothy grin, she gushed, "A princess, Mommie. A real live princess with a crown and a long shiny dress."

A princess, with a crown and a long shiny dress, huh?

"Abigail is going as a princess. Her mommie ordered her costume and she showed me a picture." Clearly dazzled by the prospects of being royalty, the child continued. "It was sooo pretty, Mommie. I want to look just like Abigail."

Ordered it on line. That figures, Rebekka told herself. There probably weren't any places in the little mountain town that sold Halloween costumes. Which meant Aimee was out of luck, because even if she could afford it, there wasn't time to order anything and have it in hand by the next evening. What to do? That was the question.

"Mommie? You didn't answer me. Can I be a princess?"

Rebekka was yanked back to the reality of the moment and one little girl who was awaiting assurance that her crown was forthcoming. How to answer her?

"We'll just have to see," she said at last. "We can talk about it over supper. OK?"

"I guess," Aimee said at last. "But I really do want to be a princess."

As she pulled together their supper of hot dogs and fries, Rebekka's tormented mind exhausted every possibility she could conceive to dress her little girl as a princess. While she'd gotten paid just that day, the balance in the account had to last them for an entire month. There were other bills to pay, and car repairs to save for. And even if she had the money, she had no way to get to a larger town where a costume store might be found.

All through supper, Aimee talked of nothing but her princess outfit, wondering aloud what color the dress might be, and how big the crown was. Her mother let her talk and tried to say or do nothing that would dash her little girl's hopes. When supper was finished and the kitchen cleaned, Rebekka decided that desperate times called for desperate measures. She settled Aimee in front of the TV to watch one of her favorite shows. Before she adjourned to her bedroom and closed the door, she adjusted the volume a little higher than necessary.

Behind the door of her bedroom, she weighed out her options. There was no use calling Judith. It would simply give the woman another opportunity to put her down. The only other person she knew in town well enough to be honest with was Patti Martin, and she wasted no time calling the pre-school teacher.

Without preamble, and before she lost her nerve, Rebekka confided in her friend the extent of the problem. "Do you have any idea how I can manufacture a princess outfit? When I was a kid, my mother would have made a cardboard crown and covered it with shiny foil and some stick-on gems, and I would have been thrilled. Something tells me Aimee wouldn't be impressed."

Her friend was quiet for so long, Rebekka feared the call had dropped. "Patti? Are you there?"

"I'm here," she replied. "Sorry. I was thinking. I've got an idea, but I'd rather not tell you what it is until I can make a phone call. May I call you back in just a few?"

"Of course, that will be fine," Rebekka said, and wondered

what her friend had in mind.

"Don't worry," Patti assured her, "one way or another, we'll get Aimee outfitted for Halloween."

Rebekka tried to read to pass the time, but after reading the same paragraph in the new mystery she'd begun a few days earlier three times over, she gave up and stared at the clock. It seemed hours later, but in reality, she knew, it had only been about fifteen minutes, her phone rang and she pounced on it.

"We've got Aimee fixed up," Patti crowed. "Crown, long shiny dress, and even a scepter, although that may be a little too much for her to handle."

"What did you do? And how did you do it so quickly? You mean just like that you were able to produce a princess costume out of thin air?"

"It's a long story," Patti said. "I'll fill you in tomorrow. Can you and Aimee be at my house at eleven o'clock tomorrow morning? I'll drive you to where the costume is."

"You make this sound so mysterious," Rebekka said. "You definitely know more than you're telling me."

"Look. Just be here in the morning, we'll get Aimee fixed up, and when you hear the story, you'll understand."

It was obvious she wasn't going to learn any more, so Rebekka offered her thanks. As she re-entered the living area, where Aimee was still under the spell of the TV, her mother made the conscious decision not to mention what would happen the next morning. The last thing she wanted was to build up her daughter's hopes, only to dash them against the rocks of disappointment.

Instead, she popped a bag of popcorn, gathered Aimee on the couch, and together they enjoyed a movie she'd found by surfing the channels. When the movie ended, as she was tucking her daughter into bed, it was obvious that Aimee was still obsessed with being a princess for Halloween.

"Don't forget, Mommie," she'd said, as Rebekka started to leave her room, "tomorrow we have to go get my princess costume."

"I know," she said, hoping her voice didn't betray any of her doubts. "I know."

Once in bed, with the lights out, Rebekka remembered the letter from the mortuary. *HOW could I have forgotten that?* Her mind had relegated the matter far back on the burner, forcing her instead to concentrate on one Halloween costume. But then, she told herself, Aimee's needs were more important and pressing than the outstanding balance on Darryl's funeral.

Then she slept.

Aimee was so anxious about her costume, it took all the patience Rebekka could muster to get through breakfast and get them dressed and on their way to Patti's house. Thankfully, she reminded herself, it was only six blocks and the weather had moderated enough that it wasn't too uncomfortable. Aimee was so excited, she forgot to complain about having to walk, and for that her mother offered up silent thanks.

When she rang her friend's doorbell, the pre-school teacher quickly opened the front door. Her face wore a quizzical expression. "I didn't hear you drive up."

Busted!

"My car's on the fritz," Rebekka said, and prayed that more uncomfortable questions wouldn't be forthcoming.

"You should have told me. I could have picked you up. Gosh, that was a long walk on a cold morning."

"Yeah," Aimee piped up, "we have to walk to school every morning." Her lower lip ran out in a half-hearted pout. "It's a long way and I don't like it."

Thankfully, Patti didn't pursue the conversation further, although her friend's eyes told Rebekka she hadn't heard the last of the matter.

"Come on through the house and we'll get my car out of the garage."

She held Aimee's hand as they made their way through the neatly furnished home that Rebekka couldn't help but admire and covet. It was the kind of house she'd always quietly envisioned when she and Darryl had dreamed about their future. "Where's Merry Beth this morning?"

"She spent the night with her grandmother," Patti replied,

as she grabbed a set of keys off the kitchen island and her hoodie from the hook by the back door. "They were going to have their own private Halloween party."

How nice that at least one grandmother cares enough about her granddaughter to have her sleep over and do something special! Rebekka made an attempt to tamp down the feelings of anger that surged through her at that moment. Darryl's mother had never once even babysat Aimee, and had made it a point to be around the child as little as possible. Around Rebekka's due date, Judith had suddenly decided to make a trip to the Holy Land, and actually was half-way around the world when her only grandchild had been born.

Lucky Merry Beth!

"So where are we going, exactly?" she quizzed her friend, as they made their way out of town. "You still haven't told me what's up."

"You know, Mommie. We're going to get my Halloween costume." Her daughter was almost trembling with excitement.

"We're going to my aunt's house," Patti said at last. "Aunt Annetta," she said, and clearly hesitated, Rebekka thought. "The costume belonged to my cousin, her daughter."

Rebekka considered the answer she'd gotten, before her friend's exact words echoed in her mind. "You said the costume belonged to your cousin. Is that a past-tense belonged?"

"Past tense is correct. I'll fill in any blanks that remain after we leave."

"Patti, I don't feel comfortable about this. Something's not right"

"Trust me," Patti said as she slowed to turn between two massive stone gateposts. "There is a story here, but nothing's wrong. I will explain later."

"Promise?"

"Promise…"

And I'm going to demand that explanation.

"This driveway is about a mile long, so don't think I'm taking you to the middle of nowhere."

Rebekka was taken by the heavily wooded setting. "Oh, look, Patti. Look at that precious little house. Is this where your aunt lives?"

The car slowed as the driver concentrated on the curves in the road, giving Rebekka a better opportunity to admire the small stone and frame cottage. "That was the caretaker's house, back when my uncle was still alive and this place was a working farm."

"It doesn't look like anyone's living there," Rebekka offered, unable to take her eyes off the little building that had so unexpectedly snagged her interest. *Never mind Patti's house, I could be so at home right there.* She knew, however, that she was fortunate to have a small, two-bedroom mobile home with very few frills and even less charm. "It's just absolutely charming."

"It's empty," her friend confirmed. "Hasn't been lived in since Aunt Annetta closed down the farm a few years ago."

She wondered why someone would shutter a working farm, but Rebekka decided to hold her questions until later. Perhaps she might learn some of the answer after she met Patti's aunt.

When the large stone and clapboard mansion sprang into view around the next curve, Rebekka's breath caught in her throat.

"Sort of grabs you, doesn't it?"

"Oh, Patti, it's so rustic but elegant at the same time. This is your aunt's house?"

"It is. This is *High Lonesome*," Patti confirmed, as she pulled under the massive two-story portico. "I've spent many wonderful times here with my cousin, Jan, and Uncle A. J. and Aunt Annetta."

For just a split second, Rebekka saw an unmistakable look of sadness cross her friend's face, and didn't believe that her eyes had deceived her. *There definitely is a story here.*

"So, Aimee," their driver asked, her voice tinged with excitement, "are you ready to go see your Halloween costume?"

Aimee was already undoing the lap belt on the car seat. "You bet. I'm going to be a princess!"

"I know," Patti said, as she leaned into the back seat to help the toddler out. "And I'll bet you're going to be a beautiful princess, too!"

41

Patti rang the bell and the door was quickly answered by a older woman in a basic black dress and white apron. "Miss Patti. You haven't been here in a couple of weeks," she said.

Before Rebekka had time to wonder, Patti said, "Emma, this is my friend Rebekka Austin and this is Aimee." She put her hand on the child's shoulder. "Aimee, can you tell Emma hello?"

After a moment of hesitation, the little girl said "Hello, Emma."

Rebekka quickly followed suit.

"So this is the little girl who wants to be a princess?"

"One and the same," Patti answered. "Which direction is Aunt Annetta?"

"She and the costume are both in the den. Why don't you three go on down? You know the way."

If Aunt Annetta and the costume are both in the den, there must not be any question that Aimee can borrow it. She breathed a silent sigh of relief. Right at that moment, she didn't think she could deal with both a heartbroken child and trying to find or make a substitute costume with only hours to spare.

"This way," Patti said, indicating the large center hall that stretched away from them. She's down this way."

Rebekka marveled at the many eye-catching architectural elements of the home that appeared even larger once inside, as she and Aimee followed Patti toward the back side of the house.

When Patti turned the corner, Rebekka glimpsed a large but cozy, comfortable room, where a large stone fireplace grabbed her eye. The blaze that burned inside was both welcoming and warm. She could see why Patti's aunt might gravitate to this space. Especially if she was alone in the big house, as it appeared she was.

At the sound of visitors, a woman rose from a wingback chair near the fireplace and turned to face her guests. Patti hurried to her side, where the two exchanged a warm embrace and the older woman brushed a kiss on her niece's cheek.

"This must be your friend and her daughter," she said, and Patti quickly performed the introductions.

Rebekka was taken with the warmness of the welcome she received, and immediately felt at ease. However, that illusion of ease was soon shattered, when Aimee responded to their host's question by volunteering that she and mommie had walked to Miss Patti's house because their car was broken.

I'm all for honesty, but sometimes this young lady takes it too far.

"We are having car trouble," Rebekka confirmed, "but it'll be repaired in a few days."

"Cars can be a headache," Aunt Annetta agreed. "I hope you'll be riding again really soon."

Patti quickly changed the subject and Rebekka gave silent thanks. "But we're here, as you know," she said to her aunt, "to transform one little girl into a magical princess for at least one night."

"Then let's get to it," the older woman said. She moved to the far side of the room and brought back a large box that she laid across the arms of her chair. When she removed the lid, Rebekka couldn't contain the gasp that escaped her lips. The dress was exquisite and there was no doubt that it was custom-made. This was so far from something off the rack, she immediately wondered if she could allow Aimee to wear anything so expensive. This was a headache she hadn't seen coming, because having seen the costume, Aimee would not want to give it up.

Patti confirmed her suspicions. "Aunt Annetta had this made for Jan and a Raggedy Ann costume made for me when we were both four years old. Merry Beth's going to wear my costume tonight."

Rebekka fingered the dress while at the same time restraining her daughter, who was already going into orbit.

"Oh, Mommie. It's soooo pretty." She hugged herself. "I really will be a princess, won't I?"

"Mrs. Bigham," she said, addressing the older woman, "surely you don't want to let this out of your possession. It's exquisite, but Aimee's not the most lady-like princess you'll ever meet."

A flash of grief crossed her face, before the woman said, "If this precious little girl doesn't wear it, I don't know who ever will?"

"Surely this dress means something to you."

"It does. I protected it all these years expecting to someday have a granddaughter who could wear it. That will never be, so it would mean a lot if you would allow Aimee to use it."

Rebekka didn't quite understand why her child wearing the dress would mean so much, but she chose to ask no questions. Instead, she said, "Thank you very much," Mrs. Bigham. "We'll gladly wear it, but we'll also return it to you in good condition." *How do I explain to Aimee that she can't run or roughhouse in this dress?*

"Why don't you call me 'Aunt Annetta,' as Patti does? Something tells me we're going to be seeing more of each other." She smiled and Rebekka tried to interpret the emotion she glimpsed behind the words. "At least I hope I'll see more of you and Aimee."

The four visited for a few more minutes, while Aunt Annetta quizzed Aimee about how she liked living in Cedar Mountain, and what her favorite color was, and about her favorite food. Her little girl was totally mesmerized, and Rebekka silently grieved, because she realized this was a reception her daughter had never gotten from her own biological grandmother. Suddenly she hoped they would see more of this woman, who wanted to be known as "Aunt Annetta."

As they left, Rebekka remembered the rent money she had tucked into her purse. She and Aimee would need to walk to the landlord's house on their way home. No way was she going to take a chance on being late with her payment. Then she remembered the letter from the mortuary, and questioned how she was ever going to find the money to satisfy that debt. Never mind the seven hundred dollar car repair estimate.

I've got no problem that two thousand dollars couldn't satisfy. Just speaking the amount made her break out in a cold sweat. The words from Patti that she heard next only increased her angst.

"I'm going to take you two home," she declared. "Walking is good, but not everywhere. And I'll come back tonight about five-forty-five to pick you up for supper at my house before we take the girls trick-or-treating."

"Oh, that's not necessary," she protested. "It's warmed up nicely and it's only six blocks. We can walk."

"Nonsense. It's no problem."

"But I need to go by my landlord's house to pay the rent for next month."

"I can drop you by there. It's no big deal."

"But I can't ask you to do that. It's out of your way."

"Look, I'm going to drive you. So remind me where Joe Barton lives. I should know, but I don't."

Deciding it was useless to protest further, she provided the necessary directions and they were soon pulling into the landlord's driveway.

"This won't take long," she promised as she got out of the car, the bank envelope clutched tightly in hand. "Mr. Barton isn't exactly a conversationalist." As she made her way up the walk to the front door, she recalled her earlier interactions with the taciturn man who owned her little trailer. She had yet to see him smile, and even when he spoke, it was like he had to pay dearly for each individual word. Consequently, when she would greet him with a "Good morning," instead of asking how she was, he would simply respond with "Yeah."

46

She rang the bell and waited. When the door swung open, she said, "Hello, Mr. Barton. I've got November's rent for you."

Always in the past, after he'd taken the money, she'd been left standing at the door while he went to write a receipt, which he brought back and handed to her without so much as a "thank you." He never inquired about any problems at the trailer that might need attention, like the leaking kitchen faucet she'd reported when she first moved in. The faucet that still leaked that morning when she had washed the breakfast dishes.

"Come in," he said, "gotta talk to you."

Rebekka wanted to bang the side of her head to be sure she'd heard correctly. He had never invited her in before, and somehow, it didn't bode well. Once inside, he ushered her into the living room, where he indicated a chair. Was she in the Twilight Zone, she wondered?

He took the chair across from her, and without engaging in any chit chat, he said, "I'm giving you a month's notice. You have to move."

Rebekka felt the impact of his words all the way to her toes, even as she questioned if she was dreaming. If so, she wished she could somehow wake up. This wasn't funny.

"Move!" Just the sound of the word made her sick to her stomach, and again, Rebekka wondered if she was dreaming. "But why?" She combed her short history with the man, searching for what she could have done to be evicted. "I've always paid my rent on time, and I haven't damaged your trailer."

This was getting scary! Where would she and Aimee go?

"It's nothing like that," Joe Barton said at last. His words blasted her back out of her own impromptu pity party, and Rebekka wondered if she'd missed something he'd said. "I got a chance to sell the trailer, so I did."

He'd sold it, without even a word of warning. "But if it was for sale, why didn't you tell me? I might have been interested."

"Could you have paid cash? Immediately?"

She had to acknowledge that cash would have been beyond her means.

"Besides, I checked you out before I rented to you. I figure you're doing good to make a rent payment every month."

What he said was the truth, but that didn't mean the words hurt any less. If anything, they hurt more, because one more time, she felt like she was dealing with her former mother-in-law.

"So how much time do I have to get out? Not until after Christmas, I hope?" To find something else that she could afford would take time, she knew. And Aimee was already looking forward to Christmas, although where Santa Claus was coming from was more than she knew right then. If she could move between Christmas and New Year's, that would be easiest.

"Sorry," the very unapologetic man sitting across from her replied. "The new owner is going to be living there herself, and you've got to be out by the end of the month."

"The end of November? Surely you're kidding?"

"Afraid not," he said. He waved the bills she'd handed him earlier. "I'm going to have to give her this money to buy you the month of November."

"You mean you're going to charge me a month's rent and put me out as well?" She was mentally processing how she was going to find the money it would take to move and post deposits. "What about my security deposit? I'll get it back won't I?"

"If you're going to live there during November, you're going to have to pay. That doesn't have anything to do with you moving. And you're getting a month's notice. Now if you can vacate by midnight tonight, I'll hand you back this month's rent and we'll call everything square today. Otherwise, it's mine. I mean, the new owner's."

"What about my deposit? Will you write me a check today?"

"I'll see that you do get your deposit back," he said. But the law gives me thirty days after you vacate to cut your check. You should have it by the end of December.

Obviously he's never had his back to the wall. Neither had she, at least not to this extent. But she had to think that if the shoe were on the other foot, she would have been more concerned and compassionate.

Rebekka left the house feeling that she'd been scammed. First the car. Then the bill from the funeral home, and now she had to find a new place to rent. How was it all supposed to be made to happen? First, however, she had to get home without showing Patti that she was upset. But how did you get evicted and not get upset?

"Sorry, I took so long," she said in apology, as she climbed into the front passenger seat. "For a change, Mr. Barton wanted to talk."

"That's okay," her chauffeur said. "Aimee and I've had a good time visiting." She looked closely at Rebekka. "Honey, is something wrong? You're white as a sheet."

"Wrong?" She hesitated, not wanting to lie, but knowing she couldn't spill her gut. If for nothing else, she didn't want to upset Aimee, who would be further troubled if they had to move again.

"No, everything's fine."

The four blocks from the landlord's house to her little trailer were the longest ever. It was all she could do to extricate Aimee and her princess costume out of the back seat, while adequately thanking Patti for all she'd done, and promising to be ready at five-forty-five that evening.

Inside the trailer, she helped Aimee place the large box on the bed, and asked her to change into her inside play clothes, before she collapsed into the very masculine, too-large recliner, in order to survey the lay of the land. For sure, the little trailer showed signs of age and wear and tear. The wallpaper was torn in several places, the kitchen faucet leaked, and the carpet, especially in the living room was long past replacement stage.

But it had also been a haven in the storm and an important component in her battle to start over. Now she was about to be homeless. Somehow, she had to find the money to have her car repaired.

For all she knew, she and Aimee might be living in that car. It was a sobering proposition.

CHAPTER THREE

FORCED TO SHARE THE STORY

True to her word, Patti Martin was in Rebekka's driveway at five-forty-five. Aimee had demanded every five minutes all afternoon how long it would be before she could put on her costume. She'd opened the box often, fingering the exquisite fabric of the gown and trying on the crown. "Oh, Mommie," she had squealed more than once, "I can't wait!" Rebekka had spent the entire afternoon worrying.

Where are we going to move? And how?

Rebekka knew that rental property she might afford was in extremely short supply in Cedar Mountain. In order to make that move, she would need a rental deposit, the first month's rent, and money to have utilities changed over. She'd raised the money to move from Atlanta by selling furniture and other possessions that she could bear to part with. Since the trailer had come primarily furnished, there was nothing with her that would convert into ready money. Then there was the question of how she would get their possessions to the new place, and their other pieces from storage in Atlanta.

An answer was no closer when she put Aimee into Patti's back seat with Merry Beth, and settled herself in the front seat, offering silent thanks that it was only six blocks to Patti's house. In an effort to keep the conversation away from herself, Rebekka purposely turned around in her seat to speak to Merry Beth.

"So… Merry Beth. Your Mom tells me you're going to be a Raggedy Ann. I always loved Raggedy Ann and Raggedy Andy."

"Yes ma'am," Patti's daughter replied. I can't wait to put it on again. I tried it on last week, and it fit sooooo good." She drew out the o's. "I'll bet I'm going to be the only Raggedy Ann in Cedar Mountain."

"I'd say there's a pretty good chance you will be. Or at least, you'll have the best looking costume of any Raggedy Ann out there."

Patti pulled into her drive, stashed her car in the garage and closed the door with the remote control, making certain her vehicle wasn't out where trick-or-treaters could see it. "You just don't ever know," she complained to Rebekka, as they herded the two would be mini-celebrities into the kitchen. "As small town as we are, we still have those who don't respect what isn't theirs." A pot of chili simmered on the stove, and the flavor of something Rebekka couldn't immediately identify accosted her nostrils and made her mouth water.

"Yummm, what smells so good?"

"Just chili. Nothing special."

"My chili never smells that good. What's your secret?"

"It's my mama's recipe, but I'll be glad to share it. Then you can compare." She turned to the two excited girls, who were already digging into their costume boxes. "Hold up," she said, but with a laugh. "First things first." She took each girl by the hand and led the pair to the breakfast table. "You sit right here. We're going to eat first. Then we'll get costumes on, and it will be time to head out." She grinned. "Aren't you excited?"

"Yeah," Aimee squealed. "I can't wait to be a princess!"

You're always a princess in my book!

"Then let's eat up and get ready." Patti placed filled bowls of chili at the four place settings. Following a short blessing, daughters and mothers dug in.

"Haven't had a chance to tell you, but there's been a slight change in plans since this morning."

Rebekka looked up. Did her surprise show? "Oh? How so?"

"In addition to our two, several more from the pre-school will be going as a group. Along with several of the other pre-school teachers. Then everybody will come back here for a party afterwards."

"That sounds interesting. But can you pull off a party on such short notice?"

"I can if you and I stay here and get ready. I didn't think you'd mind."

It wasn't that she really did mind. But it would be the first time since they'd moved to Cedar Mountain that Aimee had left her to do anything, except go to pre-school.

As if sensing her unspoken hesitancy, Patti said quietly, "She'll be fine. She knows everybody in the group." Her voice dropped even lower. "Besides, things like trick-or-treating are always more fun the more there are."

Realizing that she was outnumbered, Rebekka said, "I know she'll be fine. And she'll have a good time without mama hovering over her."

"We're finished," Merry Beth announced. "Can we get ready now?"

The two girls were soon dressed in their new personalities and were dancing excitedly, first on one foot, then the other. Long before Rebekka was ready, the doorbell rang, and the other four pre-school teachers and a group of children she estimated to be at least fifteen were waiting. Amid a symphony of squeals and giggles, and a hard neck hug from Amiee for her mother, the group left.

"We'll be ready for you in 90 minutes," Patti advised, and the teacher, who Rebekka had decided was in charge, called back over her shoulder, "We'll see you then."

Patti closed and locked the door, turned off the lights in the front part of the house, and headed toward the back. "We'll be back here in the kitchen and family room, where we can't be seen from the street. I've left the porch light turned off, which is always a signal around here that trick-or-treaters shouldn't bother the house." Catching sight of the horror on her friend's face, she hastened to add, "The whole community is pretty good about honoring that signal."

Rebekka wondered just how much work would be required to pull together a party for a gaggle of three and four-year-olds. She asked as much.

"Actually, I've got most of the prep work behind me. It shouldn't take us longer than ten minutes to finish and stage everything."

"Then why did we need to stay behind?"

Her friend's answer was one that Rebekka never saw coming.

"Because we're going to talk. You and I. For starters, you're going to tell me the complete story of your car. What's more, when you left Joe Barton's house earlier today, you weren't only completely drained of color, you were wobbling as you walked. Something's big time wrong."

I should never have let her drive me to pay the rent. HOW am I going to explain all of this?

"I don't know what you're talking about," she sputtered. "I've got car trouble and I'll get it fixed."

"Uh-uh. It ain't washing. There's something you aren't telling me."

Maybe because I'm too humiliated to tell you. And if I once give it voice, then I have to own it.

Patti reached for her friend's hands, and surprise of surprises, Rebekka didn't pull away as Patti had feared. "Listen. I'm not trying to embarrass you, but it's clear to me that you've got problems you can't handle on your own. We're a loving town." She hesitated. "Well, for the most part, anyway. When someone's in trouble, we rally around them. It's what God expects us to do."

That's sure not how it was in Atlanta! Immediately, she felt so ashamed. Darryl's fellow officers had paid for the bulk of his funeral. When she moved to Cedar Mountain, several of the men had pitched in to help transfer big stuff to storage, and to load her car. One man even took her car to a mechanic and had every system checked out and paid the bill himself.

But then there were people like Judith Austin and Joe Barton today, not to mention her principal at school, who seemed determined to destroy any remaining traces of self-respect that might remain.

"Share with me, friend. Let us help. It's what we do best."

Unable to contain the tsunami of fear and embarrassment and loathing that dominated her mind and body, Rebekka burst into tears, unable to form any words for the first few minutes. Patti let her cry. Finally her friend said, "Trust me, Rebekka. You've got friends here, if you'll just open the door for us. We'd love to help you. Because that's what God tells us to do."

The cynic in her wanted to turn away at the mention of God. She'd decided that He didn't really exist. It didn't appear He'd been there for her during the nightmare of the past few months. But a breaking heart can only withstand so much, and her heart was about to implode. In truth, she realized, if she didn't open up to Patti, there was no one else. She was all alone.

"You're right," she said at last. "I'm under the gun in so many different ways, I don't know where to turn. What's more, even if I did know, I don't have the guts to do anything. I feel like I'm suspended in mid-air without even a net to catch me."

She watched Patti's eyes check the time and knew she needed to get everything out in the open. Once she opened the floodgate, there would be no closing it.

"It's not what's wrong, but how many different things are wrong. The reason I looked so stunned at Mr. Barton's today is that I've got to move. By the end of the month, no less." She wrung her hands and got up from her seat to pace the room. She couldn't tell this story and stay still.

"Move! But why?"

"He's sold the trailer and the new owner plans to live there."

"That sounds like Joe, unfortunately. But I didn't think even he could sink that low. And the car?"

"It's a couple of things, but the repair bill is going to be about seven hundred dollars. I simply don't have that kind of discretionary cash. Mr. Goddard at the garage you recommended was very nice.

He even offered to finance the repairs over thirty days, with half-down and the balance at the end of a month."

"Couldn't do that, huh? He is a nice man, however."

"Oh, he was very nice and concerned. I sensed that when he offered credit to a total stranger. But I wasn't comfortable committing myself to paying him off that quickly, so I told him I'd just have to wait until I could save the first half of the money."

"And?"

"How did you know there was more?"

"Because you don't look empty yet. Tell me the rest, because we're soon going to have to jump on those refreshments and finish up."

Rebekka shared the nightmare of planning Darryl's funeral, his mother's refusal to help, learning that his life insurance wouldn't pay off, and then discovering she had no way to pay for the service.

"Darryl's fellow officers ponied up out of their pockets to pay the mortuary. But somehow, someway, they didn't pay all of the bill. I sure don't feel that I can go back and chastise them for that." She dropped her arms in total surrender. "But neither do I have the money to pay it myself. Especially not in light of what I've learned today."

Patti indicated the vacant space beside her on the sofa. "Sit."

Without argument, Rebekka complied. Patti reached for her hands. "Dear Lord," she prayed as easily as if she were talking to

Merry Beth, "Rebekka has been hit hard, Father. We're just asking for Your presence with her as she attempts to learn a way out of this situation. Show us how we can help her. Thank You for loving us. In Your Son's name. Amen.

Rebekka sat silent and still, savoring the awe she'd felt as her friend prayed. She couldn't ever recall a time when she'd been so specifically prayed for. Feeling that some response was expected, if not demanded, she said, "Thanks for letting me unload."

"You needed it, friend." Patti rose from her seat and headed to the kitchen. "They'll be back here in less than twenty minutes. We need to get the food on the table, but don't think this is the end of our conversation." She stopped and offered Rebekka a hug. "This is just a temporary stopping place. We'll continue this tomorrow, because you are not in this alone."

The herd of candy-happy youngsters poured through the door mere seconds after Patti and Rebekka had declared everything ready. The next hour was total chaos, while the children enjoyed themselves. Rebekka kept watching Aimee out of the corner of her eye, fearful that a chance cup of juice or a sticky cookie would come in contact with the priceless costume.

Time to wind the party down came long before the children were ready, but the adults in the group stood their ground. "It's Sunday School in the morning," Patti reminded the children. "We need to get you guys home, so your parents can put you to bed. We don't want to miss church because we had so much fun tonight."

In a matter of minutes the house emptied out, and Rebekka

wasted no time getting Aimee changed into her street clothes, and the royal raiment repacked in its sturdy box. Only then did she breathe a sigh of relief.

"I need to send that costume to the cleaners, but can I leave it with you until Monday? And if you'll give me your aunt's mailing address, Aimee and I will send her a thank you note."

"Don't worry about the cleaners. Aimee didn't have it on that long. And Aunt Annetta will enjoy a thank you note, but you're going to see her tomorrow."

"Tomorrow?" She racked her brain trying to recall any commitment she'd made for Sunday. "I don't understand."

"Tomorrow is Aunt Annetta's birthday, although she would kill me if I told you her age. She's coming here for mid-afternoon birthday dinner, and you and Aimee are going to join us. My mom will be here, they're sisters-in-law, you understand. And a couple of other relatives."

"If it's family, you don't want us here."

"Now that's where you're wrong."

"But…"

"Look, when Uncle A.J. was alive, their house was always hosting some kind of get-together. Aunt Annetta always believed there was room for at least one more at the table. We used to joke that if she saw a homeless stranger on the street, she'd pick him up and bring him home to dinner."

"Well…." Rebekka still wasn't comfortable with the prospect, but it did mean a free meal and a chance to be with other people. Adults. As much as she loved Aimee, there were times she longed for the chance to just relax with others her own age.

"Besides," Patti added, "Aunt Annetta was the one who first suggested that you and Aimee come tomorrow."

"Why would she do that? She barely knows me."

"That's just Aunt Annetta for you. Now, let me drive you and Aimee home. Sunday School time will come early in the morning."

Sunday School!

While she hadn't made a conscious decision to skip church the next morning, Rebakka knew that with their spasmodic attendance record, few would notice if they were absent yet again. In truth, given all the obstacles that had suddenly been thrown in her path, church was the last place she wanted to be.

She and Patti quickly got the two girls loaded in the car and a few minutes later, Patti dropped them at their door. "We'll pick you up for Sunday School by nine-fifteen," Patti said, as Rebekka loosened Aimee from her car seat. "Then after church, we'll go straight to my house. If you want to change clothes after church, just bring them with you."

Suddenly this was all getting so much more complicated.

"You know, Patti. The more I think about it, I think Aimee and I shouldn't…"

"You're right… you shouldn't worry about coming to Aunt Annetta's party tomorrow." She rewarded Rebekka with a wicked grin. "Now that's the end of that." Again with her trademark grin that Rebekka had found infectious on their first meeting. "Goodnight, friend. See you both in the morning."

She hurried Aimee into the trailer, and was reminded once again that their days in the little home on wheels that had been such a godsend were numbered. Where would they go? She would have to begin searching for something immediately.

Aimee was still on a high, not so much from candy, but because she wasn't accustomed to all the group interaction she'd enjoyed that evening.

"Did you have a good time being a fairy princess and trick-or-treating with your friends tonight?"

"Oh, Mommie," the little girl gushed, "it was so much fun. I was beautiful."

Rebekka had to choke back a laugh at her daughter's totally authentic ego. "Yes, my dear, you were a very beautiful princess. Now we need to get her majesty to bed, because we're going to Sunday School and church in the morning."

"Yea," Aimee said, "I like Sunday School. I wish we could go every Sunday."

Rebekka felt the heart stab way down deep. Who was she to deny her child Sunday School because Darryl's death and Judith's defection had soured her on life? She suddenly recalled Sunday mornings when she'd been Aimee's age, and was immediately remorseful. *Mama and Daddy made sure we were there every Sunday. They must be so disappointed in me.*

As she was tucking Aimee into bed, she said, "Now you know we're going to Miss Patti's after church tomorrow. If there are any of your toys you want to take for you and Merry Beth to play with, we need to take them with us when we leave in the morning.

"OK, Mommie," her child murmured, sleep already beginning to claim her. "I love you."

Rebekka's heart hurt yet again. "I love you, too," she whispered, then dropped a kiss on the little girl's head. "You're always my princess whether you're in costume or not."

The alarm sounded the next morning before she was ready, but Rebekka crawled out of bed, got her shower and dressed, then woke Aimee and they had breakfast. When Patti's husband's SUV pulled into her drive, both mother and daughter were ready and waiting. Patti hopped out to help them get loaded. Both little girls were beside themselves with excitement.

Rebakka settled in her seat and was fastening her seat belt when Patti said, "I know you've seen my husband around, but I don't think you've been formally introduced." She indicated the handsome man behind the wheel, and thinking of Darryl, Rebekka experienced a momentary twinge of grief. Or was it jealousy? "This is Bruce," Patti continued. "He finally made it in last night while Merry Beth and I were bringing you home."

She knew from snatches of earlier conversations with Patti that her husband was spending several weeks working in the south end of the state, and would soon be returning to Cedar Mountain to open a branch of his company's office. Patti had lamented how badly she and Merry Beth missed him. She hoped he would be home to stay by the New Year.

"Hey, Rebekka," the driver said and he glanced around, rewarding her with a wide, warm grin. "It's good to finally meet you. Patti talks about you so much. Thank you for being such a good friend to her."

ME a good friend to her? She talks about me so much?

"It's so nice to meet you, too, Bruce," she finally said. "But I thought it was Patti who was being such a good friend to me."

"In truth, it's a two-way street," Patti said. "Since the first day you brought Aimee to pre-school, just in those few minutes we talked, there was just some kind of connection. At least there was for me. It was almost like we were kin."

The words were sobering. Rebekka questioned if she had been so insulated in her grief and all her troubles, that she hadn't been as attentive to Patti as she should have been?

By the time they arrived at church, time for conversation had passed. The next few hours were a blur. Sunday School was a bit uncomfortable for her, because she felt on display in the small group of twenty-some class members. Worship was better, because in a sanctuary filled with more than three hundred people, she felt like she could fade into the crowd and no one would notice her.

When church was over, Rebekka found herself being greeted by first one and then another, as she struggled to make her way outside. Bruce had gone to the nursery to get both of the girls, who had gone there following the children's moment with the pastor early in the service. Patti had gone to her pre-school office to make sure everything was ready for Monday, and they're all agreed to meet on the spacious front porch of the church.

By the time she finally arrived, Bruce and the children were there. Patti could be seen making her way through the now almost empty sanctuary, and they were soon on their way to the Martin home.

After changing Aimee into nice play clothes, and seeing the two friends enjoying each other, Rebekka insisted that Patti allow her to help with the dinner preparation. As the two of them moved about the kitchen mixing and cooking and cutting and setting the table, they had an opportunity to talk.

"So you really felt like we were related the first time we met?" she asked.

Patti smiled. "I know it sounds crazy, but that's literally how it felt." Her face troubled. "That doesn't bother you, does it?"

"No, no. Not at all. I'm flattered. I never had much family growing up. I was an only child, and so were both my parents. So I had no cousins or even aunts and uncles." She paused with the cucumber she was dicing for the tossed salad. "I guess I'd just sort of gotten used to being alone like that."

When I met Darryl, that was the first time I felt like I had family. Then when Aimee came along, it just got better. Then suddenly Aimee was all I had. Now Patti says she feels connected to me.

"I have two brothers, but they both live several hours away, so I only see them about once a year," Patti explained, as she dipped the chicken breasts she was baking in melted butter and cheese cracker crumbs. "Jen, Aunt Annetta's daughter and I were very close. She was an only child and we were practically the same age, so we were more like sisters."

Rebekka finished assembling the salad and slid it into the refrigerator to chill. Patti had already said they'd serve their plates buffet style, so she didn't have to create individual portions of the green vegetable medley. "You indicated yesterday that there was a back story to your cousin and the costume Aimee wore last night." She glanced at her friend to be sure she wasn't overstepping. "I kind of got the idea it's a sad story."

As she slid the baking pan of chicken into the oven, Patti turned to her and Rebekka couldn't mistake the grief and sadness that crossed her face. She leaned against the counter. "It is sad." She motioned toward the door to the garage. "Let's step out here for a sec. I don't want Merry Beth to know this story yet. And if Aunt Annetta should come early, I don't want her to hear it either."

This must be some more story, Rebekka thought.

"Jan and I were practically the same age, as I said," she explained, as she pulled the door to the house closed. "We were inseparable. One of us was always at the other's house, but we were equally welcomed and equally comfortable either place."

She paused, and Rebekka saw clearly the grief that still lay just below the surface.

"If this is too painful," she said, "you don't...."

"No," Patti said, I'll still be this way a hundred years from now. It's not a long story." Then she paused, and wiped at a tear that Rebekka saw had come into her eye.

"When Jan was thirteen, she was diagnosed with leukemia. The bad kind. She went through a bone marrow transplant, all kinds of chemo. You name it, they did it. If money and love and attention and prayers could have saved her, she'd still be here today. But when she was barely seventeen, she finally couldn't fight it anymore." Tears that had been lurking around the edges of her eyes finally turned loose and coursed down her cheeks.

"My heart has never been so broken, not even when my dad died way too young. I felt like Jan had been stolen from me."

Rebekka was quiet, unable to say what she knew she should.

"Then a year to the day after we lost Jan, Uncle A.J. took his own life."

"Oh, Patti! Poor Aunt Annetta." Then, at the risk of sounding heartless. "First her daughter and then her husband."

"She was devastated. We all were. He was the most energetic, outgoing, prince of a guy you could ever want to know. But he felt like he'd failed Jan, like if only he'd done more, he could have saved

69

her. In the end, according to the note he left, he simply couldn't face life without her."

Suddenly the basic trappings of the garage swirled from her line of vision. Gone were the two cars, the workbench along the side wall, and the upright freezer in the corner near the kitchen door. Instead, Rebekka was seeing the Bigham mansion with a small girl dressed as a princess, racing through its rooms. She'd never seen Jan's picture, but she tried to imagine the change when those same joyous walls contained the dying in body and later in mind. The enormity was mind-boggling.

Then she remembered the princess costume. "I can't believe Aunt Annetta was willing for Aimee to wear Jan's costume. I'd think it would be part of a shrine. When I think that we might have damaged it in any way, I go cold all over." She made a mental note to carefully inspect the dress again.

"She saved everything Jan had, but she's never been obsessively protective of anything. Knowing that Merry Beth was wearing my old costume, I thought about Jan's princess outfit. So I called Aunt Annetta and asked her."

"I can't believe she agreed."

"She didn't exactly. Not at first anyway." Patti caught sight of the uncomfortable expression on her friend's face. "She wasn't negative about it," she hastened to say. "She said she didn't know if she could find it. But I know how organized she is. That was just her way of asking for time to think about it."

70

"I'm so very thankful she said yes, but I sure hope we didn't damage the dress."

"I was going to tell her I'd give her time to find it and I'd call her back. But when I told her it was for Aimee, she suddenly decided she knew where it was stored."

"But why? She doesn't even know me."

"I don't know. Aunt Annetta is always generous to a fault. And she is on the school board, you know?"

"I didn't realize she was a board member." *I don't know any of the board members. I need to make it my business to learn their names.*

"But just because she's on…"

Rebekka was interrupted when Patti's husband opened the door from the kitchen. "Honey, your chicken is starting to get really fragrant."

"Oh, my gosh." She made a dash for the oven door. "We got to talking and I totally forgot about the chicken." She yanked open the door, grabbed a mitt, and pulled the baking pan toward her. "We're good," she said, as she returned the pan to the oven and closed the door. "They need about another five minutes. But no more."

Rebekka took that to mean that conversation of a private and personal nature was adjourned. And she was okay with that. She'd already learned more than she ever dreamed she would. Now it was time to process it.

The remainder of the afternoon was a frantic, joyous blur. Several of Patti's family members came for the occasion, and while Rebekka enjoyed meeting everyone, she still found herself feeling somewhat overwhelmed. She'd never experienced a family that was so large and full of life.

One touching moment of the afternoon came after the meal, when Aunt Annetta had moved to the living room to open her gifts. Without any prompting from her mother, Aimee had approached the older woman.

"Aunt 'netta," she'd said, "thank you for letting me wear your costume. I felt like a real princess."

Rebekka had been frozen to her seat, where she was able to see the reaction on their benefactor's face. It had been, she would decide later, a combination of extreme joy and crippling grief.

"Why, darling. You're just so welcome. I'm sure you were one of the most beautiful princesses ever." From the unsaid, Rebekka knew the older woman was remembering the first little girl who'd worn the dress.

God, thank you for Aunt Annetta. While she wasn't in the habit of talking to God as if He were sitting next to her, for reasons she couldn't explain, the thanks had slipped from her sub-conscious before she was even aware of the thought.

Aunt Annetta had hugged Aimee tightly, and Rebekka also realized for the first time, how deprived her child was for family relationships such as this. She offered another quick thanks for being adopted into this family. Indeed, each and every one had made her feel so welcome.

Along toward the end of the afternoon, everyone began to drift away, including the guest of honor. Bruce had already loaded all her gifts into her car, and she was about to leave, when she summoned Rebekka.

"My dear, I just want to tell you how much you've honored me with your presence today. I hope to see more of you in the days ahead. Please feel free to drop in on me at *High Lonesome* whenever you have a chance." While her voice sounded most inviting, Rebekka couldn't decide if the look on her face was one of defeat or depression. She could easily see how either could be the case.

"And please bring that precious Aimee with you. It's been too long since my home rang with the laughter of children. I'd love to have her visit me. You've obviously done a wonderful job raising her."

Confusion momentarily overtook her, as she tried to know how to respond to the compliment. Finally she said, "Thank you for all your kindness to Aimee. She is a special little girl if I do say so myself." She reached in to hug the woman, was half-way surprised that she didn't pull back, and said, "As soon as I get my car repaired, we will come and see you. That's a promise."

"I intend to see that you keep that promise, my dear. I will hold you to that."

As Rebekka watched her sliding behind the wheel of the Lincoln parked in the front drive, she couldn't help but compare Aunt

Annetta to Darryl's mother, Judith. *Aunt Annetta has given Aimee more love and attention in two days than her own grandmother has since the child has been in this world.*

A little later, Patti delivered Rebekka and Aimee back to their place, along with enough food in disposable containers to feed them for a couple of meals.

"I've already put the word out,"" Patti declared, "you're looking for rental property. Everyone who was there today knows what we need. We'll find something. Now don't worry about it."

While Rebekka promised not to worry, she knew keeping that promise was going to be hard. She'd never had to worry before about being homeless, but suddenly she was. The prospect was most frightening.

Monday morning was there before she was ready to roll out and face the day, but Rebekka did what she considered the adult thing. She made herself get up, get ready, get Aimee fed and ready, and them out the door in ample time. There should be no need to sweat signing in on time this day.

It was, however, much colder outside, and a biting wind that cut right through didn't make the trek on foot to pre-school any easier.

"Mommie, I'm so cold," Aimee complained before they were even half way to the church. "When is our car going to not be sick?"

Her explanation when the car first failed them, had been to explain that the car was sick and had to go to the car hospital. Only that had been well over two week ago. So how did she now explain that the car was so sick, it might not get well? The answer was, she decided, to say as little as possible.

"Sometimes it takes a while for a car to get well, sweetie. Maybe later this week. But don't count on it."

"I can't walk in the cold, Mommie. My feet are freezing."

Rebekka made a silent vow right there on the sidewalk, that she would go back to the mechanic that afternoon to see if there was any other alternative type credit he could give her, so that Aimee didn't have to walk to school. In the meantime, she needed to look at her checking account and see exactly how much she could spare that day to get the work started. The problem was, she was going to have to have some money to rent another place. Could she even afford to part with anything to the mechanic? And did she have a choice? Aimee couldn't be expected to continue walking to school in the bitter weather that was only going to get worse.

In one respect, the day flew by. But in another way, it crept, feeling three days long. When she finally signed out at school, she hurried across town to the mechanic's shop, only to learn that he'd driven into Atlanta to pick up a repair part and would be gone for the day.

"I'll be back tomorrow," she told the young woman who had greeted her. Rebekka had tried to be polite, but made it clear that she had to talk with the owner.

On Tuesday afternoon, as soon as school was out, she'd hurried back to the garage where she found the owner in, but not very receptive. "I'm sorry, Mrs. Austin, but as I told you before, thirty days is as long as I can wait for my money, and I must have half up front."

She fought her emotions, defying the tears that threatened to burst forth. "I don't mean to beg, Mr. Goddard, but my little girl, she's almost four, is really struggling to walk to school each morning in these frigid temperatures. And now I've learned over the weekend that I have to find a new place to rent."

"I'm sorry, I really am. But I've been stung too many times trying to help people out of tight spots. I'll have to have three hundred fifty dollars before I can even order the parts."

What was she to do? "Alright, Mr. Goddard. I thank you for your consideration. Let me re-check my money and see if there is any way I can find another hundred and fifty that I can spare right now."

"Just let me know," the mechanic said. "I do sympathize with your plight. I wish there was more that I could do."

"Thank you, Mr. Goddard. I'll be in touch."

The remainder of the week was such a carbon copy from day to day, Rebekka found herself confused about even what day it was. The only thing she knew for certain was that she couldn't turn loose of the money necessary to repair the car, and she was no closer to finding a new place to call home. The first week of four was almost gone. Time was getting away from her every day. And she had done nothing about the outstanding bill for Darryl's funeral.

On Friday evening her phone rang. While the caller's name didn't show on Caller ID, she did recognize it as a local number.

Ordinarily she didn't answer numbers she didn't know, but on the outside chance that it might be someone calling with a lead on a place to rent, she threw caution to the wind.

"Rebekka, dear? It's Aunt Annetta. I hope I'm not calling you at a bad time."

Why is she calling me?

"No ma'am, Aimee and I are just sitting here talking about our day. How nice to hear your voice."

"I'll come right to the point. I was hoping that the two of you could come to *High Lonesome* for a luncheon tomorrow. If you can, I was going to invite Patti and Merry Beth as well."

"We'd love to come. That's very sweet of you to invite us. But I still have no wheels."

"You mean Mr. Goddard hasn't finished with your car yet? That's totally unacceptable, or it would be for me!"

She didn't want to give the mechanic a black eye he didn't deserve. At the same time, she wasn't comfortable confiding in a near total stranger that work hadn't even begun because she couldn't afford the repair bill.

"There have just been some snags, but I'm sure he'll get us going next week." She hesitated, "Could we perhaps have a raincheck?"

The silence was so long, Rebekka feared she'd offended the new aunt who had just adopted her.

"Let me call you back in just a few minutes. I've just had an idea, but I need to think about it."

Rebekka didn't quite know how to interpret that response, but knew that an answer was expected. "Certainly," she said. That'll be fine." Then she remembered her manners. "But thank you for the thought and the invitation."

It was at least fifteen minutes before the phone rang again. This time, Patti's number showed on the Caller ID.

"Hello, friend. How are you tonight? Sorry I didn't get a chance to speak when I picked up Aimee this afternoon."

"Not a problem," her caller replied. "It's been a crazy day and we've had to deal with state inspectors as well. They passed us with flying colors, but they sure do get in the way when you're trying to work with small children."

"Glad it was you and not me," she replied. "So what can I do you for tonight?" The transposed words in that question had been a standard response from her dad, and she occasionally found herself using the question without even thinking about it.

"Aunt Annetta called me. Merry Beth and I will pick the two of you up at eleven tomorrow and we'll all have lunch together at *High Lonesome*."

"I hated to turn her down, but with no wheels..."

"Did you ever stop to think that we would be going anyway?"

"Okay, I guess that one slid right by me. But it's my turn to chauffeur you, and I can't make that offer."

"There'll be plenty of time after you get your car back. Don't worry about it."

After she'd put Aimee to bed that night, Rebekka sat down with her checkbook and the bills that had to be paid, including her storage unit rent. When she finally saw the total of uncommitted money left until her next payday, her heart fell into her shoes. *It doesn't matter which way you slice it, there's simply not enough money left to repair the car, pay to rent a new house or apartment, and still buy groceries for the remainder of the month.*

As she crawled into bed, exhausted, physically, emotionally, as well as financially, one last thought flashed through her mind. She hadn't included the funeral bill in her list of payables.

"Oh, God, what am I going to do?" she whispered, as she clutched the covers, feeling like she had to have something to anchor her.

This is so not fair!

CHAPTER FOUR
WHAT DO I WANT FOR CHRISTMAS?

It took everything she had to make herself put on a false front for the luncheon at *High Lonesome*. For Aimee's sake, she made the effort. Otherwise, she told herself, she would have stayed home, in bed, with the covers pulled over her head.

Instead, she and Aimee were ready when Patti arrived. Once at the estate, she was captivated again by the sheer rural beauty of the setting, and the comfortable ambiance of the house. However, nothing could have been warmer than the welcome they received from the lady of house. The cherry on the sundae were the table decorations and the menu of child-friendly foods, with ample helpings for adults.

This meal was planned with the children in mind. I'm impressed.

The luncheon was truly a magical time, and their hostess made sure to engage in conversation with her youngest guests, which gave both girls a feeling of importance. Rebekka couldn't have been more proud of how Aimee conducted herself.

When finally the dessert dishes had been removed and they were ready to leave the table, Aunt Annetta suggested that Aimee and Merry Beth might like to spend some time in the playroom on the second floor.

"Trust me," she said to Rebekka and Patti, "there's nothing in there that they can hurt, and more importantly, there's nothing in there to hurt them. This way we can talk, as soon as I get back from getting them settled."

The two of them made their way into the huge den where again, a warm and inviting fire was blazing merrily on the hearth.

"I could absolutely live in this room," Rebekka offered, as they selected seats being careful to leave the wingback closest to the fire for their hostess. "I don't think I've ever been in a room so homey and inviting." She glanced around at the various decorating elements. "To be so large, it sure is cozy."

"I've always thought that the personality of this room was just a copy of the person who lives here. This was one lively place when Uncle A.J. was alive."

"That it was," said Annetta Bigham, as she made her way to

her chair.

Rebekka found herself embarrassed that they'd been overheard, but Patti's demeanor was anything but regretful.

"Remember the Christmas parties we used to have in this room when Jan and I were both children?" She looked wistful for a moment. "You should have been here for some of those, Rebekka. Uncle A.J. would hire a professional Santa to "drop in," meaning that he never had to drop out of sight. Both Jan and I probably believed in Santa two of three years longer, because we saw him here."

"Those were some wonderful times," Aunt Annetta agreed. "And you know what? I think we're going to hold that party this year. Merry Beth and Aimee are at the prefect age to make the night special, and we'll get Santa to pay us a visit as well."

"Oh, Aunt Annetta," Patti cautioned. "It's been over ten years since you threw that Christmas party. Do you think you can?"

"That last one was the first Christmas after Jan got sick in October. Always after that, she didn't have the strength and her immune system was so fragile, we didn't dare expose her to a lot of people."

"I remember."

Rebekka sat quietly, fearful of intruding on what was obviously a special but painful memory for the two women bound by blood and loss. Finally, however, the lady of the manor spoke. "If I have the party, probably on Saturday night before Christmas, would you and Aimee be in town?"

"Oh, yes, we'll be here."

"So when will you go to be with your family? I don't want to knock you out of that trip?"

Rebekka hesitated, unsure of how much to share with this woman who, while she was still a near stranger on the one hand, was so very comfortable and familiar at the same time. Finally, she said, "We have no other family. Both my parents died several years ago, and I'm an only child. All my grandparents are gone as well."

"I know that you're a recent widow. Patti told me. I hope you'll accept my condolences. It's not an easy road to travel. I know, and now you do, too."

"Thank you," Rebekka said, fighting the urge to tear up. "I never knew I could miss anyone as much as I do Darryl. But missing him won't bring him back. So Aimee and I are making our own way now."

Missing him may not bring him back, but would the funeral home disinter him if I don't pay them? Without fail, I've got to see about that on Monday.

"What about his side of the family? I can only imagine that Aimee's other grandmother will be over the moon to see her at Christmas? When will you visit her?"

Again, Rebekka found herself between the proverbial rock and the hard place. How should she answer truthfully without trashing Judith? Fortunately, Patti came to her rescue.

"Rebekka is too nice to tell you the truth, Aunt Annetta." She flashed an "I've got this…" expression. "Darryl's mother never accepted Rebekka. She had very little contact with Aimee before Darryl was killed, and absolutely none since."

"Do you mean to tell me that precious child has a grandmother who doesn't think the sun rose and set in her?"

"I'm afraid so," Rebekka said. "It absolutely breaks my heart, and I've tried everything I know to bridge that gap. Not for me, but for Aimee. So far, nothing."

"I'll never have a grandchild, but I would give everything I have for that blessing."

The conversation continued for the next hour, as Aunt Annetta asked about Rebekka's growing up years, how she was liking Cedar Mountain, and if she thought she would settle in the community, or was her job at the school just a stepping stone to something else?

"I'd love to settle here. Right now, however, I'm desperately looking for another place to live. I have to vacate by the end of the month, and I'm no closer to finding something than when I started."

"But my dear, you've got that cute little mobile home. It looks just like you and Aimee. I would have thought you'd be very happy there."

"It's not Rebekka," Patti interrupted to say. "Joe Barton has sold the trailer to someone who plans to live there. She just found out last week."

"Gracious! What're you going to do? Rental property isn't that prevalent here in Cedar Mountain, I'm sorry to say."

"It's very hard to find. Especially at a price I can pay. But somehow, there has to be something out there for us. It's just so nerve-wracking going to bed every night knowing that I'm another day closer to my move out date, and I still have nowhere to go."

"We'll pray about this, my dear. And I'll make some calls. I know several people who have property they don't openly advertise."

"Thank you, Aunt Annetta. You don't know how I appreciate it." She looked at Patti. "Don't you think we need to get those girls home?" She glanced at her watch. "It's already after three-thirty."

"We do have to go, Aunt Annetta. Bruce is coming in early tonight, and I want to have a good meal on the table for him. We'll get to eat as a family for a change."

"You take care of that Bruce; you hear me? That boy's a keeper."

"You've got that right."

"But before you go, let's talk Christmas again for just a second. You all need to let me know what I can get each of the girls, because I don't want to duplicate what Santa might get them. For that matter, I'd love to know what each of you wants. That goes for Bruce, as well," she said.

Annetta Bigham looked at Rebekka and said, "Tell me dear. If you could have anything you want, what would it be?

The question caught the young woman off guard. She had the answer, but wasn't sure she should be so bold with someone she barely knew. Finally the words just bubbled up inside her and had to come out.

"There are actually three things that I would ask Santa to bring me. First would be a permanent home, preferably a house, for Aimee and me. Second would be a family. After seeing all of you last Sunday, I realized that Aimee doesn't have any idea what it means to be part of an extended family. And third and last, I'd love to have the security of knowing that I can provide for me and my child going forward."

"That's an ambitious wish list."

"It is that," Rebekka confessed. "Naturally, I don't expect you to supply any of those items. But if you would really like to get me something I'd enjoy, I'd love a gift certificate to a book store. I haven't bought a new book since before Darryl died. I can't justify spending the money."

That last part just slipped out, and the minute the words left her mouth, Rebekka harshly chastised herself for being so open with this woman she'd only known for little over a week.

Almost as if she hadn't heard Rebekka's outlandish wish list, the older woman said, "A gift certificate to a book store. You shall have one, my dear. That's a promise from me and Santa."

"Did you know that Rebekka is a publishing writer?"

Aunt Annetta sat straighter in her chair. "That's wonderful. I'd love to read some of your work."

"I'm just getting started," Rebekka protested.

"Don't belittle yourself. Every successful writer started small and at the bottom."

The three visited for a few more minutes, before gathering the children and heading back to town.

Everything was low-key for both mother and daughter. Patti insisted on driving them to church on Sunday, and before she knew it, or was even ready, it was Sunday night. The next day was Monday, and that meant school and the usual routine. The walk to pre-school and work the next morning was especially brutal, and she questioned how much longer she could subject one little girl not yet four years old to such a harsh journey each morning.

During class later in the morning, her cell phone vibrated. She glanced at it, and saw the number of the mechanic who was holding her car hostage, because it wouldn't move under its own steam. However, she was in the middle of a discussion on the difference between the American stage and European stages of the twentieth century, and elected to ignore the summons.

At her planning period, she returned the call. "Mr. Goddard, I saw where you called me, but I was teaching at the time and couldn't answer. I apologize." She didn't want the man to think she was deliberately ignoring him, but figured he was calling to tell her if she wasn't going to have the repairs made, he'd have to charge her storage.

"That's alright, Mrs. Austin. I understand. Listen, we need to talk about your car."

Yep, here it comes.

"This whole thing has been heavy on my heart and my mind. I know that you're struggling, and it's been laid on my heart to see if I can help you."

"Help me?"

"Yes ma'am. I know teachers don't make a lot, and it's just you and your little girl. And now you say you've got to move. Do you mind telling me why?"

Rebekka didn't think it was really any of his business, but neither did she want to appear rude. So, in twenty-five words or less, she shared that her rental home had been sold.

"So you're moving because you have no choice?"

"Yessir. My daughter and I have been very happy there, but the new owner plans to occupy it."

"Then tell me if this will work for you. I can start work on your car tomorrow, and you pay the first half of the money at the end of the month. You pay the second half at the end of December, and just between us, if you need into January, because that pretty little girl of yours is going to have to have Christmas, I guess we can manage that."

Rebekka couldn't believe her ears, and was actually struck dumb for a few seconds.

"Mrs. Austin? Did I lose you?"

"What? Oh. No. Oh, Mr. Goddard," she babbled, "you would really do this for me?"

"Yes ma'am, we can make this work, and I should be able to have you up and going by Friday, maybe even Thursday. But better you plan on Friday."

Oh, thank you, Mr. Goddard. God bless you. I don't know what else to say."

"I've already been blessed, Mrs. Austin. Trust me, I have."

The remainder of the day was almost like a dream. She had to pinch herself to be sure she wasn't dreaming. When she collected Aimee from pre-school that afternoon, she didn't even wait until they were home to share the news.

"Oh, Mommie. You mean we won't have to walk in the cold any more?"

"We'll still have to for the next two or three days for sure, but by Friday, we should have our car back. Won't that be wonderful?"

I wonder what changed Mr. Goddard's mind? But she decided to not look a gift horse in the mouth, and gave thanks instead that one hurdle was behind her. It would still be a stretch to find the money to pay him, but she would find it. Somehow.

As the week rocketed toward the middle of the month, the task of finding a new place to live was making as much progress as it had. Nothing was happening. She'd lost count of the number of phone calls she'd made inquiring about property. What was out there was either entirely too big, much too small, so that they would be sharing a bedroom of eighty square feet, or it was buried in the boonies. What few perfect places she'd found were far beyond her budget. Especially with the car repair and the outstanding funeral bill.

True to his word, Mr. Goddard called at lunch on Friday to say the car was ready, he'd already road-tested it, and that she could pick it up any time before five-thirty that afternoon. As soon as she could get out of school, Rebekka headed to the garage, where in the span of a few short minutes, she and her car were reunited. It had been so long since she'd slid under the steering wheel, she actually questioned for a minute if she even remembered how to drive.

Before she left, she pulled out her checkbook and offered to make a good-faith payment toward the six hundred ninety-one dollar repair charge. But Mr. Goddard refused to accept it.

"We agreed at the end of this month, when you get paid, and then again at the end of December."

"Thank you, Mr. Goddard." She had to stifle an impulse to hug the man and give him a kiss, but she decided she didn't know him quite well enough for that. He trusted her to pay him what she owed. That was enough, and she vowed she would get him paid and on time.

Driving off in the car was like being in the presence of a favorite aunt that you hadn't seen in years. Aimee was equally thrilled to walk out of the church to find their car waiting.

"Oh, Mommie. I thought our car would never get well."

"That makes two of us, honey."

On Saturday, with only sixteen days until they had to be out, Rebekka ran through a couple of liquor stores and picked up empty boxes to use for packing. She also scoured the FOR RENT ads in the local paper, searched on line, and even called every real estate agency in town, asking if anyone handled rental property. The two leads she got fizzled just as quickly. One was a basement apartment in a house in town, but the owner, who lived upstairs, had a strict rule about no children. The second piece was priced more like a mortgage payment than a rental price.

Not knowing what else to do, she loaded up Aimee and the two visited the three motels in town, to see what kind of long-term rental price she could negotiate. The idea of living in a motel room, and of having to eat every meal out, wasn't an attractive option. But neither was living in their car, and at that moment, the motel room won hands-down.

It was after church the next day, when Patti and Bruce approached her on the church front porch, where she'd just come from collecting Aimee from the older children's nursery.

"Hey," Bruce said, "I hear you got your car back. I hope it's working okay?"

"It seems to be," she assured them. "And I am more than glad to get it back. Bless Mr. Goddard's caring heart." She was determined to let everyone know what a compassionate man he was.

"We've got a proposition for you," Patti ventured. "How about you drive your car home, and we'll follow. We want to take you and Aimee out to lunch, then we've got a surprise for you both."

"A surprise? I'm afraid I don't understand."

"You will when you see it," Bruce assured her. "But let's go. If we don't hurry, the Methodists will get to the buffet first, and they pick it clean like a hoard of locust."

"Oh, Bruce. You're exaggerating. It's nothing like that, but it does make us stand in line longer."

"Then by all means, let's get on the road." As she headed toward the little trailer, knowing her days of going this familiar route were definitely dwindling, Rebekka couldn't help but wonder what kind of surprise they. Aimee was just so happy to be with Merry Beth, she didn't question the surprise part.

The line wasn't too bad at the town's favorite home-cooking restaurant, and the five of them were soon seated and eating. Everyone was quiet for the first few minutes, but as food disappeared from their plates, the tempo of the conversation picked up.

"Guess what?" Patti said. Then before Rebekka could even devise an answer, her friend exclaimed. "Bruce's commute and his distance from us is about to come to a halt a good month earlier than we'd thought. When he comes home for Thanksgiving, he won't be going back to south Georgia. On the Monday after Thanksgiving, he'll begin opening his own office right here in Cedar Mountain."

Rebekka looked from one to the other. "Hey guys, that's really great. I'm so happy for all three of you. So this is my surprise, and how great it is to be able to celebrate."

There was no missing the look that passed between husband and wife. Finally, Patti said, "No friend, we've got a surprise just for you and Aimee."

"So tell me what it is."

"Nope," Bruce said, "our lips are sealed until we get there. And you won't even know where we're going, because Patti is going to blindfold you and both of the girls. This is going to be a true surprise."

Rebekka couldn't begin to imagine what was in store for her, and it was obvious that her hosts intended to divulge no additional information. Suddenly it became extremely important that dessert be eaten quickly. As her mother had been fond of saying, curiosity killed the cat. And she felt like she was racing through her nine lives quickly.

It had been a long time since she'd been surprised. Pleasantly surprised, anyway.

When they got to the car, Patti produced three strips of black cloth, which she tied over both girls' eyes, and then, taking extra care, made certain that Rebekka could see nothing.

"Now listen girls. This is a game. If you can play by the rules and keep your blindfolds on for just a few minutes, we can go afterwards and get ice cream. But you can't take off your blindfold until I tell you. And when you see where we are, don't say anything until after Miss Rebekka's blindfold is off."

Gosh, this is getting complicated.

"Do you understand, girls?"

A chorus of yesses came from the back seat, and Bruce put the SUV into motion. Rebekka tried to time the distance, but was having little luck. She couldn't even decide which direction they were traveling. She would go along with the game, but she'd also be glad when she could see again.

The vehicle slowed, made a left turn, and she could tell they were driving at a much slower speed. The road was very curvy. And then they stopped. Patti said, "Okay, girls, let's remove your blindfolds first. But remember, don't say anything." She stepped to the back and unmasked each girl. Rebekka heard them giggling. "Remember," Patti cautioned. "You can giggle, but don't say anything."

At the same time, Bruce said, "Here, Rebekka, give me your hand and I'll help you out." She did as ordered, and after a little stumbling, found herself standing on solid ground.

"You can remove your blindfold any time you're ready," Patti said.

Rebekka fumbled with the knot in the back and ended up pulling the black piece of cloth off over her head. What greeted her eyes was nothing like what she'd expected.

She was standing in front of the small stone and frame cottage on the grounds at *High Lonesome*. The former caretaker's home.

"And this is my surprise how?"

"It's your new home, silly." Then almost as if she feared she'd hurt Rebekka's feelings, Patti said, "That is, if you want it."

Rebekka had moved up onto the porch and was peering in through a window at what appeared to be a roomy country kitchen. "You want to explain this?" she asked.

Bruce took the lead. "We'll answer all your questions, but first let's get inside, before these two girls get too chilled." He pulled a key from his pocket. They all trooped inside, where they found it was a little warmer. At least the biting wind outside wasn't a factor.

"Here's how it plays out. Aunt Annetta would like to rent you this cottage for whatever amount you're paying in rent now. And she will pay the utilities as well, but you'll have to provide your own furniture."

"But how? Why?" She hated to question what clearly was a godsend, but suddenly she was feeling overwhelmed.

"Remember, Aunt Annetta is a giver. That's what she does. This cottage is just sitting here deteriorating, because there's no one living in it to help preserve it. It would be a win-win for both of you."

"Come on," Bruce said, "let's look at the rest of the place, so you can better make up your mind."

It didn't take long to see the two small bedrooms that were larger than what they had in the trailer. The one bathroom was good size, and had washer-dryer connections. *No more lugging clothes to the laundromat!* The living room was the largest room in the house, and it had a large, stone fireplace that Rebekka could immediately visualize in use. *I can literally feel the warmth.*

What excited her the most, however, was the small ell off the living room. She wasn't certain of its intended purpose when the house was built, but she knew exactly how she would use it. Even without measuring, it appeared to be the perfect size to hold her desk and file cabinets. There was space for her bookcases in the living room itself. Plus the large window that looked out onto the heavily-wooded landscape at *High Lonesome* literally brought the outside in.

Talk about inspiration to write!

Back in the kitchen, she inspected the stove and refrigerator that were older, but appeared to be clean and in working order. There was adequate cabinet and work space, more than she had in the trailer, and the floor space was large enough to hold a table and chairs without crowding.

"Well?" Patti asked.

"I love it," Rebekka gushed. "But how do we do this? How do we make it work?

"Okay, here's the deal," Bruce said. "This place is going to have to have some work. Aunt Annetta will put the guys in here as soon as you can select your paint colors and any other decisions that need to be made."

"But you have to be out in two weeks, and that may be pushing things just a bit," Patti added. "After all, you can't possibly select paint colors until after you get out of school tomorrow. So here are your options. You can go to the new owner of your place and see if you can purchase an additional week into December. Or you can vacate on time, store your possessions in one of the outbuildings here, and you and Aimee can bunk in with us for a few days. We're not talking but a week at most."

"But... but..."

"And, here's the rest. When you're ready to move, some of the guys from the Sunday School class to lend us their backs and arms and legs. We'll go to Atlanta and clean out your storage unit and bring everything back and set it into place."

Suddenly Rebekka had heard all she could handle without losing her composure. As the tears began to stream down her face, she attempted to talk, to make Patti and Bruce understand that they were tears of joy and relief and happiness. Finally, she was able to get that message across.

"So you're going to take it?"

"Oh, yes, Patti. Oh yes. Most definitely. But I need to hug Aunt Annetta's neck." She called to her daughter, who was in the other part of the cottage with Merry Beth. "Aimee. Come in here."

A head stuck around the door. "Yes, Mommie?"

The child crossed the room, and Rebekka knelt down to eye level and asked, "How would you like for this to be our new home? You could have all those things that were in your room in Atlanta here. Would you like that?"

"Of course, Mommie. We heard you and Miss Patti and Mr. Bruce talking. I've already shown Merry Beth where my bed is going to be, so she can come and spend the night with me."

Out of the mouths of babes!

They quickly secured the house, loaded up, and Bruce drove them on to the big house, where one anxious Aunt Annetta was waiting. When Rebekka spotted her, she promptly forgot all her reservations and ran to embrace the woman, who met her with open arms.

"May I assume you're going to take the cottage?"

"Oh, yes, you better know it!"

"You know it's not as modern as some other places you might get."

"Modern doesn't have charm. That cottage is just the right size for the two of us, but even empty and cold like it is right now, there's a coziness that we won't find anywhere else."

"Then we'll consider it a deal, and we'll get the workmen in there as soon as you can give me some choices and colors."

"Really, I'm just a renter. Whatever you select, I'm sure we'll be happy."

"Nonsense," the older woman said, "if that's going to be your home, you need to decorate it so that it will go with your furniture and so that you can feel happy and at home there."

"I'm not believing this."

"My dear, I can't visualize anyone else in that little house. I hope you'll be half as happy there as you've made me this afternoon."

Rebekka hugged her again, and the Aimee had to get in on the act. When Aunt Annetta straightened from the hug Aimee had given her, she excused herself. When she returned, she handed Rebekka a sheet of paper. "This is a list of every decision we need made. Here's a list of the places you can go to look at swatches and samples. Make your choices and get back to me and we'll get underway."

They parted soon after, and when Rebekka and Aimee were dropped at their door, Rebekka found herself unable to tell her good friends how grateful she was.

"It's okay," Patti said, "it's been that kind of afternoon for us as well."

After supper, after she'd put Aimee to bed, Rebekka got out the list and began to study all the decisions that confronted her. Before she was even half through the list, her brain was swirling worse than a tornado in Kansas. But she did have mind enough to estimate that if she didn't have to pay utilities or storage unit rent in Atlanta, that would at least allow her to pay off the funeral bill. And since she didn't have to pay security deposits on the cottage, she would be able to pay off the car repair bill.

It was with a greatly relieved mind that she dropped off to sleep. But not before she made herself a note to call the mortuary the very next day. The longer she ignored them, the less likely they were to work with her on payment terms.

Tomorrow was going to be a new day.

CHAPTER FIVE

DECISIONS

I t truly had been a new day! But as she was crawling into bed that night, sore both of mind and of body, Rebekka could only conclude that if ever there had been a day that deserved the label "Monday," this day had been it!

Aimee had been so tired from the weekend, she hadn't wanted to abandon her comfortable bed. As a result, her mother had found herself signing in at school mere seconds before the time changed to seven-thirty-one. Mr. Hawkins had made certain she understood how close to the wire she'd cut it.

Evidently her students were as out of it as Aimee had been that morning, because they didn't want to get with the program, either. She'd had to send two students to the principal's office as a result, then had her lunch ruined when the mother of one of the students came to challenge her.

As she was about to clock out, thankful beyond words that the school day had finally ended, she noticed the sign beside the computer that proclaimed... MANDATORY FACULTY MEETING 3 p.m. Rebekka racked her brain, questioning how she'd missed such a large sign that morning. Only after she was finally seated in the library, did she learn by overhearing other conversations that the meeting hadn't been posted until almost lunch.

Not only was she more than ready to leave the dust of the school day behind, but the list of stops and decisions she needed to make was burning a hole in her tote bag, thanks to the delay. There was no way she was going to get it all done.

Finally, the meeting began. The principal addressed the issue of the upcoming Thanksgiving and Christmas holidays and how student testing would occur around those dates. He cautioned teachers that there would be no excused absences for faculty on the last day of class before either holiday. He ended with a comment Rebekka felt was directed totally at her.

"Let me remind you again," he said, "if you sign in after seven-thirty, it becomes a disciplinary matter. Yet morning after morning, I see teachers signing in at seven-thirty." He paused and glanced around the group, but Rebekka felt his eyes bore in on her. "In an ideal world, by seven-thirty you would already be in your classroom, getting ready for students to arrive.

"When you don't sign in until seven-thirty, you're actually

cheating the school system and the students." He looked her way again. "Let's see going forward what we can do to make this a more ideal world and me a happier principal."

He paused again, his eyes swept over the group, and he said, "That is all. You may go."

It took everything Rebekka had not to trample the other faculty members getting to the door. On all the mornings she'd been right under the wire signing in, she'd seen no other faculty nearby. Evidently the principal had used that occasion to target her, and the anger she felt almost made her want to hand him her classroom key and tell him to go take a flying leap.

However…

There was the little matter of a contract she'd signed, not to mention a daughter who depended on her to make sure she was fed. And there were bills. In the end, she settled for escaping the building to concentrate more on their new home and less on her principal's happiness quotient.

A quick glance at the clock on the car dash confirmed her suspicion that she'd lost a good forty minutes. There was no way she would be able to cover all the bases that afternoon, and still be able to get Aimee from pre-school aftercare by five o'clock.

What was she to do? Should she put off shopping and give it a fresh go tomorrow? Aunt Annetta needed to know her choices as soon as possible. And besides, she didn't want to wait another day to begin. For the first time in her life, she had a house that was practically going to be hers. She was excited to decorate it.

In the end, she decided she had no other choice than to prioritize. With the list of work in hand, she attempted to reason out what would have to be done first. Those decisions had to be at the top of her errand list. Which was how she ended up at the paint store selecting a foggy pale, muted gold color for all the walls in the cottage. The painting had to be done before any floor work. So that decision was made. Tuesday was for all the remaining decisions.

Aunt Annetta had plumbing and electrical work on the list, but she decided she needed to know more of what was required of her. She'd ask when she called her new landlady later that evening. Then she was on her way to claim Aimee, sliding in just two minutes before closing, which would have cost her an additional fee.

Whew! Seems like I've been almost late for everything I've done today!

Once home, she and Aimee made quick work of supper. Then she called *High Lonesome* to ask if they might drive out. Her answer was a quick and enthusiastic 'yes!'. "Why don't you come eat with me," Aunt Annetta had suggested.

"That's sweet of you, but we've already eaten. We got home this evening, and both of us were famished."

"I'll see you when you get here," Aunt Annetta said, as they ended the call.

Rebekka made quick work of grabbing her lists, the swatch for the paint color she'd chosen, and her questions.

"Come on, Aimee. Let's go see Aunt Annetta."

As she swung between the gateposts and made her way along the curving drive, when the cottage… HER cottage came into view, she couldn't help but stop still in the road to take it all in.

"Why're we stopping, Mommie? Aunt 'netta's waiting."

I know, sweetie. But aren't you excited about us living here? Mommie just had to stop and look at it for a minute."

"Uh-huh. But I wanna see Aunt 'netta."

Knowing when she was outnumbered, Rebekka moved on past the quaint little cottage, promising herself that she would count the days before they could begin living there.

You know it's going to be farther to town each morning. How are you going to handle that?

As much as the musings of the voice behind her left ear startled her, she refused to let it dampen her enthusiasm for their new home. She would handle it somehow, and she would get to work by seven-thirty, never mind Mr. Hawkins.

Once in the den at *High Lonesome*, she wasted little time sharing the color she'd chosen for the walls. "This color makes me think of sunshine, and I think it will look good throughout. Then we can leave all the dark-stained woodwork just like it is."

"My dear, I'm so pleased with your selection. I agree that it's perfect. And leaving the woodwork alone will make the job go faster.

But I will have the painters clean and polish all the trim."

Rebekka explained about the late start that afternoon, but promised to get back on it the next day. She did, however, inquire about the plumbing and the electrical work.

"Really and truly, you don't have to worry about most of that. In fact, I'll call those men right now and tell them we're ready for them as soon as they can get here. We need them out before the painters go in."

It felt good to see some of the items disappearing off the list.

"Now you will need to select new light fixtures, and new appliances for the kitchen. There isn't a dishwasher there now, but why don't we put one in, especially since we have the plumbers and electricians there anyway?"

"This sounds like it could get expensive," Rebekka pointed out. "I don't mind doing without a dishwasher. But I would like a washer and dryer."

"Rebekka, my dear, you need both a dishwasher and that washer and dryer, so get all of them."

Gosh, is this what it feels like when you have a fairy godmother?

"And what about the floors? What are you thinking? Carpet?

This was a subject that she had debated as well, and finally Rebekka said. "I don't know what it would cost, but those beautiful old wide plank floors are too pretty too cover with carpet. They don't look that bad. Couldn't we refinish them, then get some pretty area rugs instead of wall to wall carpet?"

Aunt Annetta rose from her chair and grabbed the poker to punch up the fire. "I like the way you think. You and I are on the same page, although if you'd wanted wall-to-wall carpet, I was fine with that."

"I'd rather have the beauty of the floors."

"Tell you what. I'm sure there's no insulation under those floors. If you're going to keep the bare wood, we need to insulate the crawl space. I'll add that to my list."

Before they left, Rebekka was given her own personal key to the cottage. "You come and go as you need to," she was told. "That's your house. Go inside whenever you like, and don't think you have to ask my permission."

Back at home, she got Aimee bathed and into pajamas, and they sat down to talk about their new house. Suddenly, as homey as the little trailer had been, it paled in comparison to the cottage that was about to replace it. Rebekka would always remember the mobile home as the place where she took the first tiny step toward a new life, but she would leave it with spirits high.

As she tucked Aimee in to bed, she told her. "In the morning, and every morning, whether we want to or not, we have to get up in time for Mommie to be at her job on time. Remember, when we move to the new house, we'll have to drive into town."

"I know, Mommie," the little girl agreed, as Rebekka planted a kiss on her head. "You better let me get to sleep so I can wake up on time tomorrow."

Almost four one minute and almost forty the next. This kid doesn't miss a trick.

As she readied herself for bed, she thought again about how much Aimee was missing because Judith refused to make room in her life for the little girl. *She doesn't even have to speak to me, if only she would be a grandmother to Aimee. I guess God sent Aunt Annetta in Judith's place.*

The remainder of the week went at a fast clip. When Rebekka and Aimee went by the cottage on Wednesday night, it was evident that plumbing and electrical work was underway. Both Tuesday and Wednesday afternoons had been devoted to looking at more samples of everything imaginable, but by the end of the day on Wednesday, every decision on the list had been made. She breathed an exhausted sigh of relief. She was running on fumes, but it felt so good.

The following week, school adjourned after classes on Monday for the Thanksgiving holiday, and Rebekka said a silent prayer of thanksgiving ahead of time for the break in her hectic schedule. It also meant that she was at the cottage two or three times a day. Every time she saw something new, evidence that progress was being made, she rejoiced and checked the calendar to see how many more days remained to finish the renovation.

Thanksgiving Day dawned frigid and bright. An arctic cold front had descended on the mountains, and it was impossible to set the thermostat high enough in the trailer to keep them comfortable.

Both Aimee and her mother were dressed in heavy sweats indoors, and had to pile on even more layers when they went outside.

Aunt Annetta had invited them for Thanksgiving dinner. Patti and Bruce were going to his family's get-together, although they'd promised to drop by later in the afternoon. All of the other extended family had plans, so it ended up being just the three of them at *High Lonesome*.

As soon as they were in the den, Rebekka had backed up to the huge fire and allowed the warmth to almost bake her back side. "Oh, if only I could put some of this good heat into a five gallon bucket and take it home with us. The furnace in our little trailer just can't stand up to these frigid temperatures."

"You know you and Aimee are more than welcome to stay here with me. I can't bear knowing that you're cold and uncomfortable there."

"We'll be fine," Rebekka assured her. "They say the weather is supposed to moderate by mid-day tomorrow."

"You should be fine for heat and air in the cottage. I had that new unit installed less than a year before the last people moved out. It's barely been used."

"I'm sure we will be," Rebekka assured her. "I just can't wait to spend our first night there."

"I'm as anxious as you are."

Because it was just the three of them, and because the day

was so very cold, Emma had set up a table and chairs in one end of the den, and it was there, amongst the objects of art, the warmth and charm of the wooden moldings and gingerbread, and near the warm fire that they enjoyed a traditional Thanksgiving meal, complete with pumpkin pie and pecan pie for dessert.

"Oh, man, am I ever stuffed." Rebekka rose slowly from the table, unable to move as freely as she might have liked. "I'll bet there's nothing in my closet that's going to fit come tomorrow morning."

"Mommie? Can I go to the playroom? I'll be good. I promise."

"You'll have to ask Aunt Annetta, darling. Remember, you're a guest here."

"Sweetheart, you go right on up to the playroom. Can you turn the light on by yourself?"

There was nothing like the grin of a precious, innocent child, Rebekka thought.

"Yes ma'am, I can turn it on myself. I'm almost four years old, you know."

"I'd heard that you were almost grown, so you go on to the playroom and enjoy yourself. As soon as Merry Beth arrives, I'll send her on up."

They both watched as the little girl left the room and headed to the stairway to the upper floor.

"We're spoiling her, you know."

"And your point would be what?" Aunt Annetta asked.

"That I think she deserves at least a little spoiling. Thank you for being in her life what a grandmother would usually do."

"The pleasure is all mine, believe me."

Rebekka struggled to find a comfortable position on the couch, where her over-stuffed tummy wasn't taxed. "It may take me until tomorrow to get over this meal. For sure I won't need any supper."

"So what do you have planned for tomorrow, I mean since there's no school?"

"Mostly I'm going to be tying up a lot of loose ends, and getting ready to hand back the key next week. It's hard to believe that we're just days away from moving out."

"Time flies. I certainly can attest to that."

"That it does.

They spent the remainder of the afternoon visiting, and Rebekka shared about her growing up years, and how she and Darryl had fallen in love. When Patti and Bruce arrived, they joined the conversation while Merry Beth headed to the playroom. It was well after dark before the group broke up. Back at the trailer, Rebekka suggested that Aimee sleep with her, since her bed had an electric blanket that could keep both of them warm.

And warm they were. So much so that crawling out from under the covers the next morning was about like walking barefooted across solid ice. Rebekka had left the thermostat higher than normal, but it was still frigid in the little trailer. Both mother and daughter decided not to shower, and instead pulled on the warmest clothes they had. This would be a Thanksgiving week for the record books, at least as far as temperatures went.

Rebekka suggested that they go out for breakfast, where they could get some hot food served in warm surroundings. Aimee was up for it. After they'd finished their Belgian waffles and hash brown casserole, Rebekka laid out the plan for the day. She needed to zip out to the cottage to measure a wall for a piece of furniture. Then, she promised, the two of them would go to the indoor mall in the next town and shop.

"We may not buy a lot," she explained, "but we can shop and look all we want."

That's when her daughter hit her with a question she hadn't anticipated. "What are we giving Aunt 'netta for Christmas? She asked me what I wanted."

Oh, my gosh. I hadn't even thought that far ahead. What do you buy someone who has everything? For that matter, what is Santa Claus going to bring Aimee? She realized that at almost four years old, for probably the first time, Christmas would be very important to this little girl. She and her classmates would be comparing notes all the way up to the big day, which only made it more of a priority.

"I don't know darling. We'll have to talk to Miss Patti and see if she can give us some suggestions."

114

"We have to get her a nice present," Aimee advised, in a most solemn voice.

"We do, and we will. What did you tell her you wanted?"

"A doll house. And furniture."

"A doll house? I've never heard you talk about wanting one."

"There's one in the playroom. It's real big. Bigger than me. But I don't need one that big."

That must have been Jan's doll house. I'm sure she and Patti both played in it. She made a quiet note to herself to check out the doll house the next time the opportunity presented itself.

"Well, I hope you won't be too disappointed if Aunt Annetta gets you something else. Even a small doll house would be a really big gift. So don't get your hopes up. Promise me?"

"I promise, Mommie. I can always play with the one in the playroom."

Her little girl was growing up. At least at this particular moment. Rebekka knew that the almost four-year-old could return at any moment. And probably would. It was also obvious that she already considered herself a welcome visitor to the mansion, a visitor who didn't need an invitation. But then Aunt Annetta had that effect on people.

With her head already brimming with ideas and questions about the cottage, Rebekka pulled into the drive by the kitchen, they got out, and hurried up onto the porch. The wind was still biting and the cottage promised some warmth. Even though their errand shouldn't take more than five minutes, it would feel better doing it out of the cold. The workmen had taken a long Thanksgiving weekend, and wouldn't be back until Monday. Which meant she and Aimee could putter in the house without being in the way.

The minute she turned the lock and pushed the door, Rebekka knew something was wrong. Always before, the door had swung in with almost no effort at all. This time, despite her pushing, there seemed to be something holding it. She wondered if something had fallen on the floor in front of the door. Cupping her hands around her face, she peered through one of the panes in the top half of the door. What she saw shot fear and dismay straight through her. She looked again, to be sure she wasn't seeing things that weren't actually there.

The entire floor appeared to be a solid sheet of ice. How that could be, she didn't know. But she was certain she wasn't imagining things. It was equally certain that she wouldn't be able to get the door open by herself.

"Come on, Aimee. We need to see Aunt Annetta now."

Her little girl had been wandering about on the porch, jumping off and walking back up the three short steps, only to jump off again. "What's wrong, Mommie? Why aren't we going in?"

"I just need to talk to Aunt Annetta first. Let's you and me run on up to her house. You'd like to see her this morning, wouldn't you?"

"Yeah, I love Aunt 'netta."

Rebekka took the curves probably faster than was safe, but something was bad wrong in the cottage. Her cottage. And while she wasn't totally versed in house problems, something told her they had big trouble."

She swung the car to the rear of the house, and rang the back doorbell, knowing that Emma would be in the kitchen. Sure enough, in less than a minute, the smiling face of the long-time domestic swung open the door.

"Miss Rebekka, Miss Aimee. We weren't expecting to see you two this morning." She stepped aside. "Here, get in here out of that cold. Can I offer you come hot chocolate?"

Bebekka looked over her daughter's head and caught the housekeeper's eye. "Aimee, why don't you let Emma fix you some hot chocolate, while I visit with Aunt Annetta for a minute? Then when you finish getting warm, you can come on into the den."

Emma had gotten the silent signal. She nodded her head in the direction of the den. "Come on, Aimee. You can help me make the hot chocolate. Would you like miniature marshmallows or big fluffy marshmallows that look like little pillows?"

As she took off down the hall, Rebekka heard her daughter say, "I'd like some of both, please."

At least she remembered to say please!

As she rounded the doorway into the spacious living area, she could glimpse the lady of the manor in her wingchair reading.

"Aunt Annetta," she squawked, suddenly unable to speak clearly because she'd been running so fast.

"Rebekka. It's so good…" She hesitated, and studied her guest closely. "Something's wrong. Come here, dear. Sit down and tell me what's brought you here so early this morning and in such a state."

Now that the floor was finally hers, Rebekka found herself momentarily tongue tied, uncertain of how to begin.

"The cottage, Aunt Annetta. I can't get the kitchen door open, and the entire floor looks like a skating rink. It's a solid sheet of ice."

"My dear. Are you sure?" Then before Rebekka could reply, she said, "Well of course you're sure, or you wouldn't be here." She reached for her phone. "Let me see what I can do."

When her call was answered, Rebekka heard Aunt Annetta explain what appeared to be a problem. "Thank you, Mr. Thompson. I hate to break into your holiday weekend, but this sounds serious." She appeared to be listening. "Yes, just come on up to the house when you've finished. Rebekka and I will be waiting here where it's warm."

She ended the call and turned to her distraught visitor. "Gary Thompson is a peach of a guy, and he'll be right out to see what we've got going on. In the meantime, we might as well relax and wait for him."

"I guess," Rebekka said, already bummed out by what was happening. It didn't matter what the problem was, it was going to affect when she could take occupancy, and that posed several problems.

"I know, my dear," Aunt Annetta said as if she were reading her mind. "It's probably not good news, but whatever it is, we'll deal with it. It's as simple as that."

Before Rebekka could reply, they both heard a voice from down the hall, "Aunt 'netta, I've come to see you." Aimee came racing into the room, still sporting a chocolate milk mustache.

Annetta Bigham turned and held open her arms, and Aimee ran straight into them. They each hugged.

"There's no one I would rather see first thing this morning than you and your mother."

"Really, Aunt 'netta?"

"Really, my dear. You both have become very special to me."

Aimee squirmed loose from the embrace. "Can I go up to the playroom?"

The playroom. The doll house!

"You surely may," Aunt Annetta said. "You know the way."

"Yes ma'am."

"Why don't I walk up with you and then I'll come back down and visit some more with Aunt Annetta?"

"Okay, Mommie. Then I can show you the doll house."

Rebekka immediately thought of her mother's two of many sayings: little pitchers have big ears and if a child knows it, she's gonna tell it.

"That was Jan's doll house," Aunt Annetta said quietly. "I think it would make her happy to know that Aimee is enjoying it so much." She turned to Rebekka. "Walk on up with her, dear. Perhaps by the time you come back down, we'll have heard something from Mr. Thompson."

Taking her daughter's hand, Rebekka allowed Aimee to lead her up the stairs and to the large playroom on the back side of the house. Aimee stood on tiptoe to reach the light switch, and immediately, the room was flooded with brightness. While she'd been in the room once before, Rebekka hadn't really paid attention to all the different toys and activity areas. It truly was a child's wonderland. No wonder Aimee and Merry Beth loved playing here.

"Here Mommie. See. Here's the playhouse." She pointed toward the far end of the room, where a small house in miniature took up the entire space. It appeared to be about half size of a regular house, and the area around was covered by green carpet. Silk flowers and plants softened the landscaping, and the entire scene literally screamed "Come and play in me!"

"It is beautiful, darling." Then a thought hit her. "You know, this belonged to Aunt Annetta's daughter, and I'm sure it and everything in this room are very special to her."

"I know, Mommie."

"You're a lucky little girl to get to play in here whenever you want, but you must promise me that you will be very careful not to damage anything. Will you promise me that?"

Aimee tugged at her mother's hand. "Come look inside. I love this doll house."

She allowed herself to be led, and true to Aimee's prediction, the interior looked as if it would be a perfect home, if only it were full size. Nothing had been spared in the construction.

After Aimee showed her several other favorite toys, Rebekka left her to play and returned to the den, where she found Aunt Annetta reading by the fire.

"That is absolutely the most exquisite playhouse I think I've ever seen."

The older lady looked up from her book. "That was all A.J.'s doing. He would have done anything for Jan." She hesitated, and Rebekka saw the pain that momentarily captured her friend's face. "That's why it hurt him so much when she died. He felt like, somehow, he'd failed her."

Rebekka said nothing. What, she wondered, was there to say? Obviously, the wound was still fresh enough to cause pain even after the passing of time.

"That's why I'm so happy to see Aimee using the room," the woman continued, as if she hadn't noticed Rebekka's lack of a response. "Several times I've considered dismantling the room and doing something else entirely up there. But I couldn't ever bring myself to take that step. And now I don't have to."

Rebekka was about so speak, when Emma stepped into the room. "Mr. Thompson is here. Would you like for him to come on back?"

"Yes, please, that will be fine. And would you bring us some coffee?"

Rebekka braced herself, questioning if she was ready to hear the bad news and at the same time wondering how it was taking so long for the man to get there. Before she could chastise herself further, a tall, stocky man dressed in clean khaki coveralls and holding a bill cap in his hands, joined them.

"Mr. Thompson. I am so very grateful to you for coming out this morning. I will of course pay you for your time and trouble." She turned to Rebekka. "I don't think my friend here, Rebekka Austin, has been at the cottage when you were there. She's going to be my tenant, and she's the one who found the problem this morning."

"Good Morning, Ms. Austin. It's so good to meet you." His voice sounded like sweet honey with a touch of a twang that Rebekka couldn't identify. He turned to his employer. "It's a good thing Ms. Austin did come out this morning. If this had gone undetected until Monday, I shudder to think what it would be like."

"Then we have major problems." Aunt Annetta's words weren't a question, but a declaration.

Rebekka froze. Was it possible she wasn't going to get to live in the cottage at all? How major did problems have to be to make the house unlivable?

"We have major problems," Mr. Thompson said. "Fortunately, they aren't insurmountable."

"Please," Aunt Annetta said, "where are my manners? Let's all sit at the table over here." She indicated a gaming table in the corner on the other side of the fireplace. "Then you can tell us everything we need to know."

Once they were seated, the contractor took the floor. "Ms. Austin was correct. The floor throughout the entire house is coated in a sheet of ice about half an inch thick. The water soaked into the bottom of the kitchen door, swelled it, then froze, and that's why it wouldn't open."

"But where did the water come from?" Rebekka asked.

"Something happened to the central heat sometime after we left on Wednesday. We're going to have to get that checked. With no heat, a water pipe in the bathroom froze and burst. Water poured out, flooded the entire house, and when the temperatures dropped so low last night, it did what water does. It froze."

"So this translates to what?" Aunt Annetta asked.

"I've turned the water off outside the house. We've got to get the heat seen about and do whatever has to be done to get it working again. In the meantime, we've got to repair the ruptured pipe and check for any other possible ruptures that we can't see. Then once the heat is back on, the ice will begin to melt. That's when we'll have to be there, at the ready, with wet vacuums to remove the water as fast as it melts."

Rebekka thought of the beautiful wide, old hardwood boards that were the floor throughout. She already had large area rugs selected to place under the furniture in each room.

"Are we going to lose the hardwood floors? Am I going to have to go back with carpet instead?"

The prospect of carpet was a downer, but if it had to be, it had to be.

"Those floors are chestnut boards almost an inch thick. Fortunately, the temperature was cold enough that the water froze almost as soon as it hit the floor. The ice actually saved the floors. But we've got to get it off of there immediately, as soon as it turns back into water."

"Then tell us where we go from here."

"The good news, Mrs. Bigham, is that I have already put out an SOS to the heating people and the plumber. They're both on their way now. I've also called for a couple of my crew to come begin the clean-up." He gave Rebekka what she interpreted as his reassuring smile. "We'll get it all put back to rights."

"But will you be able to have the house ready for me by Friday? I have to be out where I am by midnight that night."

He rubbed his chin. "Now that, Ms. Austin, may be a problem. May be, I say, because it's too soon to tell how much of a delay this has caused."

"What am I going to do?"

Aunt Annetta put her hand on Rebekka's. "Let's don't panic, my dear. And let's don't borrow trouble." She turned to the contractor. "Mr. Thompson, how soon do you think you'll be able to give us an idea of where we stand?"

He fingered his chin again. "Perhaps by the end of today, but more realistically, lunch tomorrow."

"Then we shall wait until tomorrow, and then we'll draft a plan of action." She squeezed Rebekka's hand. "It's not the end of the world, you know. You and Aimee are most welcome with me here if we're delayed."

Rebekka couldn't decide if it was the uncertainty of where she was going to live and when, or the fact that she'd had her heart set on being able to live in the little cottage much sooner, rather than later. As she looked around the den at *High Lonesome*, taking in the dark wood moldings, the paneling, the autumn colored walls and furnishings in hues of red and yellow and gold and orange, it hit her. Without meaning too, she'd used the mansion as inspiration for the color choices she'd made for the little house in the woods.

Now it looked as if the only way she would get to live among those colors in the next few days would be to move in for the short term at *High Lonesome*.

This was all certainly not going as she had envisioned.

CHAPTER SIX

A TROUBLING CHANGE OF PLANS

Once Mr. Thompson left, after promising to give them an update at the earliest possible moment, Aunt Annetta had turned to Rebekka. "As I said, dear, you and Aimee are most welcome here. Go ahead and plan to vacate the trailer on schedule. You'll definitely have a place to lay your heads." She wrung her hands conspiratorially. "And I, for one, will take extreme delight in having others under this roof, even if it is only for a few days."

Rebekka hugged her. "You're too good to us, you know? But I thank you for it."

"God tells us to do unto others as we would have them to do unto us. I have no doubt, my dear, that if the situation were reversed, you'd be offering me a place. And I have so much, so many blessings. God expects me to share them, just like He gave His Son to us."

Rebekka left with tears in her eyes, and a lump in her throat. But in her heart, she knew she'd just seen a sermon lived. It was something that would stay with her forever, she said aloud to the car.

"What did you say, Mommie?"

She'd totally forgotten that Aimee was in her seat behind her. How much did the child hear? How should she answer?

"I was just saying how nice Aunt Annetta has been to us. We're very fortunate, you know?"

"I love Aunt 'netta. And she loves me. She told me so."

She showed me! After so many months of fighting to survive, being bad-mouthed by people, many of whom were under the influence of Judith, it was so empowering to know that someone believed that you had worth.

The urge to go shopping had long since left her, and it appeared that Aimee had forgotten as well. But there was somewhere she had to go, and she made the decision to do it that very day. Instead of going home, she pulled into the parking lot at The Green Spot grocery and pulled out her phone.

When Patti answered, Rebekka got right to the point. Patti immediately agreed. "How would you like to spend the day with Merry Beth?" She asked Aimee, as she ended the call.

"Oooooo... really Mommie. Can I?"

"Miss Patti says to bring you right on over. Merry Beth is as excited as you are."

She dropped Aimee, stopped to fill up her tank, and hit the road. It was a hard two hours to the mortuary in Atlanta. She'd kept forgetting to call them, but it was a matter that had to be dealt with. And there was no time like the present.

When she pulled into the parking lot at the funeral home, Rebekka noted the absence of cars. Translated, there was no service going on this day. Just as she had hoped. She asked to see the manager, whose name escaped her for the moment. She'd worked with him on Darryl's arrangements, but that had been then. She'd slept in the interim.

"Mrs. Austin," the man said as he filled up the doorway, then entered the office. "Please don't tell me you have need of our services again so soon?"

"No, Mr. Maxwell." She'd made it a point to take a close look at the name tag he wore over his heart. "I just want to try to conclude our old business, and give you some money toward the outstanding bill on my husband's service." Fearful he'd thought she planned to pay the entire amount, she hastened to explain.

"I can't pay in full today, as much as I'd like to. But what I can do is give you a payment and my promise to pay it off within the next sixty to ninety days."

He regarded her with a quizzical look that she didn't quite

understand. Desperate for things to go her way, she prayed his silence meant acceptance. If he demanded everything she owed, there was no way she could make that happen. In which case, she might have been better off to have spoken to him by phone. But here she was, front in center, before the man she owed, and she prayed God would be with both of them. Again she had unconsciously called on God.

"Just a minute; let me see." He turned in his seat to the computer and began to tap the keys.

"What I owe you is $1,431.22." Then she realized it had been a while since that last bill. "Although I'm sure interest on the balance has made it more." Desperate to keep him from having her thrown into debtor's prison, she said quickly, "But I can pay you three hundred dollars today." She reached into her purse and pulled out her checkbook and began to write the check.

"Just a minute, Mrs. Austin."

Interpreting his command as a refusal to accept the three hundred, she babbled, "It's all I can pay right now. I've also got a large car repair bill, and it is Christmas in a few weeks. My daughter already has her list started of what she wants."

"No, you misunderstand," he said, as he pulled a sheet from the printer beneath his desk. "You've paid your bill in full." He studied the document. "In fact, it appears that we actually owe you a small refund."

Rebekka had heard the phrase "Twilight Zone Time," and right at that moment, she understood exactly what it meant. There was no way possible she could have settled that account. And it wasn't a matter of forgetting. She hadn't had the money. Plain and simple.

"I assure you, there's a mistake, Mr. Maxwell. As much as I would love to see this debt paid in full, I've given you nothing. I haven't had it to pay with."

He studied the print-out again. "According to this, we received a cash payment from you a week ago today, for the full amount we'd billed." His fingers hit the keys. "But it also appears we failed to credit the contributions from one of your husband's fellow officers. The account was actually overpaid by one hundred and twenty-five dollars."

Cash. Last Friday. Overpaid!

"Mr. Maxwell, I assure you. I was in Cedar Mountain all day last Friday, and I most certainly did not pay you any amount of cash. You can't pay what you don't have."

"Well, all I know is that according to this recap, you owe us nothing, so I'm not going to accept your money. Put your checkbook away."

This was all so bizarre.

"Are you sure you haven't credited another customer's payment to my account in error? There has to be a reasonable explanation for this."

He held up one finger, picked up the phone on his desk and punched a couple of keys. "Maxine," he said, when the other party answered. "We evidently received a payment last Friday on the Darryl

Austin service?" He was quiet. "You do remember it. Now do you recall any of the details? Who made it? How?" He was quiet again. "Mrs. Austin's in my office now, but says she hasn't paid anything on the bill, so we're confused." More silence on their end. "Yes, if you would, please."

Confused doesn't begin to describe it!

He turned to Rebekka. "Maxine Morgan is our office manager. She's on her way down to tell us what she knows."

When she left there a few minutes later, Rebekka truly was confused. According to the office manager who'd taken the payment, a well-dressed man had walked in saying he was there to pay off the balance owed on the Darryl Austin service. He didn't know how much it was, but when Mrs. Morgan told him, he'd pulled out cash and paid the bill in full.

"If the man hadn't been dressed in a suit," Rebekka had explained, "I might think it was one of Darryl's former co-workers. Had you sent them a bill as well?"

"No, ma'am," Maxine Morgan had responded. "We didn't. Yours was the only name and address we had, and you are the widow."

"I didn't reach out to them, either" Rebekka had explained, "so I don't see how they could have known there was a balance owing. But I am going to find out, because if it was them, I need to thank them."

Back in her car, she consulted her phone and quickly punched

132

in the number for Captain Hunsaker's private line. When she had him on the phone, and the two had exchanged pleasantries, she got right to the point.

"As awkward as this is," she explained, "after all of you contributed, there was a balance owing on Darryl's service. But when I got to the mortuary, they say the bill has been paid in full. A man in a suit walked in last week and gave them cash."

"That sounds like something out of a novel," the captain said.

"That it does," she agreed. "But is there any way someone from the department did that good deed? I need to thank somebody."

"Mrs. Austin, I'll ask around, but at this point I'm going to say we had nothing to do with it." He was quiet for a second. "However, I wish you had let me know, we could have helped you somehow."

"Nonsense," she protested. "You all did too much as it was, and I'll always be grateful."

He inquired how she was liking Cedar Mountain and how Aimee was, before they ended the call. All the way back to the mountains, she replayed the scenario over and over, and by the time she crossed the city limits sign, she was no closer to knowing her benefactor's identity. All she knew with any certainty was that she no longer had that debt hanging over her.

Unless all of this is a dream and I'm going to wake up to a very painful reality!"

She swung by the store and carried groceries to the trailer, before she went to collect Aimee. The temperatures outside had moderated somewhat, and she was relieved to find the icy edge gone from the temperatures inside their little home on wheels.

When Aimee was in hand, and despite Patti's demands that they both stay for supper, mother and daughter were back at home, where she fixed Aimee's favorite meal of "busketti" and meat sauce. Then they settled down to watch TV for the remainder of the evening.

As she was settling down for the night, Rebekka made a decision to call Mr. Barton the next morning to assess the possibilities of being able to buy an extra week in the trailer from the new owner. And with that, she was soon asleep.

Saturday morning dawned dark and foggy and Rebekka lay in bed longer than would normally have been the case. Aimee wasn't stirring, and she decided this might be her only chance for a week or more to sleep in. Consequently, it was after nine o'clock before her feet hit the floor. She immediately noticed that it didn't feel like she was walking barefooted across the ice. That made her think of the cottage, and she wondered what Gary Thompson's verdict was going to be.

But first things first. Before she lost her nerve, Rebekka grabbed her phone to call Mr. Barton. He answered on the seventh ring, and she'd almost given up hope of catching him.

"Mr. Barton, Rebekka Austin here. I hope you had a good Thanksgiving."

"It was just another day here, Mrs. Austin. Is that all you

needed?"

"No sir, I need to know if there's any way I can buy an additional week here."

"No, afraid not. I'll need your key on Friday."

"But Mr. Barton, the house I'm supposed to move to had the heat go out, pipes froze, and the entire house flooded."

"That's not my problem, Mrs. Austin."

"No sir, I didn't mean to imply that it was. But it's going to probably take another week to get everything repaired and ready. I don't expect to get the extra time for nothing, but otherwise, I've got to move twice, and I don't know where we're going to stay."

"That's what they make motels for, Mrs. Austin. We have three nice ones in town."

Rebekka had placed the call with high hopes, but this man's attitude was quickly getting to her. "But Mr. Barton, how do you know the new owner wouldn't be agreeable? I wish you'd put my situation before him, or her, whoever the new owner is. Or give me their name and number, and I'll call them."

"Do I look like Directory Assistance, Mrs. Austin? Your request is not only out of line, it's denied. Now is there anything else before I hang up? And remember, I'll be there next Friday at five o'clock to collect your key."

"Will you refund my deposit at that time?"

"We've already had this conversation, Mrs. Austin. The law gives me thirty days to refund a deposit, and I obey the law. Why I've never even had a parking ticket. Your check will be cut on December 30 and not a day before."

"But in that case, what with the New Year's holiday, I won't even get my money until sometime in early January. I'm a single mother, Mr. Barton. Can't you show me some compassion?"

"I'm not the post office, you know. How long it takes to deliver your check isn't up to me. You might talk to them, see if you can hurry them up. And as for compassion, that's for weaklings. If you're going to function in the adult world, Mrs. Austin, you need to buck up. I'll see you Friday at five."

There was a loud click, and the line cleared.

He hung up on me. HE HUNG UP ON ME!

Rebekka couldn't decide whether to be red hot with anger or give in to her emotions and drop into a deep blue funk. Either way, there were things to do that day, and Aimee was still asleep and they hadn't had breakfast. Before she could make a decision, her phone rang. Certain it was Mr. Barton who had had a change of heart, she answered without checking the Caller ID.

"Yes, Mr. Barton?"

"Rebekka?"

It wasn't Mr. Barton. *Aunt Annetta!*

"Yes, Aunt Annetta?"

"You must have been expecting a call from him."

"No ma'am, not exactly. I just hung up from a call with him, and I assumed it was him calling me back."

"As in calling you back to tell you he had reconsidered and you could have more time?"

Man oh man, did she nail me to the wall or what?

"That's about the size of it, I'm afraid."

"My dear, don't worry about this. I've already told you, there's a place here for the both of you until we get all of this sorted out."

"I know, but..."

"Listen, Joe Barton has been a thorn in people's sides forever. That man is perpetual gloom and doom, and most of it, he creates. Get out of there, give him his key, and come stay with me. You deserve better than having him wipe his muddy boots on you, and that's what he's doing. I've known him forever."

"We'll see," she said at last.

"Anyway, Mr. Thompson is due here in about an hour to give me a status report. I don't know what you have going this morning, but I thought you might want to be here."

Rebekka made a split second decision. "We'll see you in an hour."

She hurried to wake Aimee, who still didn't want to wake up

until she learned that a trip to *High Lonesome* was on the agenda. "But we have to hurry," Rebekka explained. "We've got to get our baths, eat breakfast and get out there, all in an hour." She didn't think it could happen, but almost an hour later to the minute, she pulled to a stop in the back drive at the mansion. They'd bathed and dressed, and she'd run through a fast food drive-through and they had eaten in the car on the way.

I don't see Mr. Thompson's truck. I must have beaten him.

As she and Aimee were getting out of the car, a red extended cab pickup truck with Thompson Construction emblazoned on the side pulled in near her.

"Good morning, Ms. Austin," the driver said as he stepped down from the cab. "Are you ready to hear what all we've found?"

"More than ready, Mr. Thompson. I just hope it's good news."

"A mixture of both, I'd venture to say." He reached into the truck and grabbed his satchel. "Shall we get on in there and see what we've got. I'm going to need some answers before we can go forward."

His words didn't inspire Rebekka to believe she and Aimee would be living in the cottage by that time next week. Still...

Once Aimee had headed to the playroom, and she and Aunt Annetta and the contractor were gathered back in the den, Mr. Thompson wasted no time getting down to the basics.

"For starters, the part needed for the furnace is on back-order.

It probably won't be here until Tuesday of next week. Perhaps as late as Wednesday."

"Then you can't do any work in there until the furnace is working, which means we're at a dead standstill until you have heat," Aunt Annetta said.

"Not exactly," the contractor said. "We can get all the repairs made. My men and I are accustomed to working without a source of good heat. Where it brings us to a screeching halt is with the finishing work. All the painting, for example. Refinishing the hardwood floors. Renewing the woodwork."

"I don't understand," Rebekka said. "Looks like working with no heat would be impossible, yet you say your men can do that."

"It has everything to do with the temperature that we need to finish. We can't roll paint on walls, if those walls are going to be cooler than thirty-two degrees. And the projected high for the next five days isn't predicted to be above twenty or twenty-two."

Rebekka started to speak, but Mr. Thompson's hand went up stop-sign fashion. "I could put portable heaters in there that would bring the temperatures above freezing. But as cold as it is, just because it's thirty-five degrees six feet away from the heater, doesn't mean it won't be twenty-eight over in the back corner."

"So you're saying we need to wait on all the finishing tasks until after the furnace is repaired. Am I hearing you correctly?" Aunt Annetta asked.

"That would be my recommendation and really my demand."

He looked across the table to Rebekka. "Ma'am, I know this throws a monkey-wrench in your plans to be moved by the end of the month, and I'm sorry."

"If we wait," Aunt Annetta said, "how long will it take you to get the house ready so Rebekka and Aimee can begin living there?"

"I figured you'd ask that." He pulled a small fold-over calendar from his pocket, flipped it open, and began to study it. "It will be Tuesday evening before that part even arrives, and that's best case scenario. Bullock's Heating & Air will jump on it as soon as we have the part in hand, which means we're looking at sometime Wednesday before the unit will be operational. And it will take several hours of continuous heat to get those walls warm enough to accept the paint."

In other words, don't plan on spending this weekend in your new home!

"It will take us three days, at least, possibly four, to complete every item on the list." He checked the calendar again. "To be on the safe side, don't plan on moving until at least a week from Tuesday. Wednesday might be better." He smiled at them both. "If we can make it happen any faster, we certainly will."

"Then if that's the best we can do," Aunt Annetta said, "that's the best we can do." She turned to Rebekka. "I'm so sorry, my dear. I wouldn't have had this happen for anything, but as you already know, you won't be homeless. You and Aimee will be right here with me."

A troubling thought crossed Rebekka's mind. "So what

happened to the heat, exactly? Is this something we're going to need to worry about happening again?"

The expression on the contractor's face betrayed his surprise that she had considered such a problem.

"A two-dollar relay switch failed. Why? We'll never really know, but I suspect it was caused from the unit not having been run in a while. And that switch caused a major component of the heating element to run continuously, until it burned up both the element and the fan motor."

Rebekka didn't totally understand the explanation, but she understood enough to know that something as simple as a wonky two-dollar part was causing her major inconvenience and many headaches.

"As far as this happening again, I'd classify it as highly doubtful." One at a time, he looked at the both of them. "Are there any other questions? I need to get back to my guys and be sure we've got what work we can do underway." He rose from the table, grabbed his hat and stuck it on his head, and made for the door.

"Thank you, Mr. Thompson," Aunt Annetta called to the man's retreating back. "Keep us posted."

The two women sat in silence and the crackling of the fire on the hearth nearby was the only sound for ever so long. Rebekka was loathe to break the quiet of the moment, because she already knew that when she did, she would begin to cry. Breaking down in front of Aunt Annetta, after this woman she'd only known for a few weeks had been so kind and generous, would make her appear ungrateful. Nothing could have been farther from the truth.

"Then it's settled." The older woman stood and put her hand on Rebekka's shoulder. "You know, you two could start staying here tonight. There's no need to stick it out in the trailer if you're uncomfortable there."

It wasn't that she didn't appreciate the offered hospitality. She did. Very much. But before she could feel safe about opening her mouth to say what was on her mind, she first had one very big obstacle to conquer and overcome. She'd become so anxious and excited about moving into the cottage, the realization that it wasn't going to happen that way, had spawned a huge amount of broken-hearted disappointment.

Somehow she had to stop acting like someone Aimee's age, she had to stop pouting, and accept what she couldn't change. Only it wasn't easy.

"I appreciate your offer," she said at last. "And we may well start staying here before the end of next week. But I've still got packing to do, and several loose ends to tie up. So we'll go on back to the trailer for now." She rewarded her benefactor with what she hoped was a sincere smile. "Besides, we're supposed to get a warming trend beginning late this evening, so maybe the worst of the cold is behind us.

I sure hope so! This weather has really put a crimp in all my plans.

142

The one thing she didn't share with Aunt Annetta was the matter of her furniture in storage in Atlanta. If she left the contents even one day into December, she would have to pay for the entire month. And while finding the money for that wasn't the issue it might have been a few days ago, the prospect of paying for an entire month simply chafed.

Things are not as dire as they were, but I still don't have money to waste.

Back at home, Rebekka settled Aimee in her bedroom playing with her dolls, and she dropped onto the couch with the legal pad in her portfolio notebook that went everywhere she did. She needed a punch list or she was going to forget something important. At the top of the list was the question about what to do about the storage unit. As she kept listing matters that needed her attention, she vowed as soon as she'd completed her list, she'd call Patti.

As much as she'd enjoyed having the week of freedom, she'd missed seeing her friend each day. Part of her would actually be glad to see Monday come, but the other part of her dreaded the return to organized chaos. Before she could add another item to her list, her phone rang.

Patti!

"Hey, why don't you and Aimee come to supper tonight? Nothing fancy, I promise." Then her voice dropped a couple of octaves, almost as if she were imparting a deep, dark secret. "Besides, we've got a surprise for you."

Another surprise?

"A surprise? I'm afraid I don't understand."

"No biggie. Just a surprise. Come eat and find out."

A troubling and suspicious thought struck her, as she remembered a movie she'd seen recently, and Rebekka couldn't keep from saying what she thought. "You aren't by any chance going to fix me up with a man tonight, are you?" Before she'd left Atlanta, no more than six weeks after Darryl was killed, people had already been playing matchmaker. She hadn't wanted it then, and she certainly didn't want it now.

"Where did that come from? Is that a subtle way of telling me you want me to find you a man?"

"When I'm ready, and that's not saying I ever will be, I can find my own man."

"Why would you even think I'd be up to such?"

In the movie she remembered, people had been invited to dinner, then found themselves confronted with an eligible man. She explained it just that way.

"No bachelors or husband-wanna-be's tonight, I promise," her friend said. "Do you think I'd actually bring in a stranger when all we're having is left-over potluck?"

"Just wanted to be sure. Yeah, we'll be there. I need to talk to you all anyway. What time?"

"Come about six and we'll have all evening."

Later that night, over beef stew and corn on the cob, Rebekka brought her friends up to date on the status of the cottage. "So you see, there's no way I'll be able to move in next Friday."

"That's not a problem," Bruce said, "you're more than welcome here."

"You're right. That's not a problem. Aunt Annetta has said we can stay there as well." She lifted her hands in a helpless gesture. "But what do I do with my stuff in the trailer? And more than that, if I don't empty my storage unit by the end of the day next Friday, I'll have to pay for the entire next month"

"That's not a problem, either," Bruce informed her. "Let me go make a couple of calls."

While he was gone, Rebekka cornered Patti. "Okay, now what about that surprise." She didn't want to admit it, but curiosity was about to get the best of her.

"Well, Bruce wanted to be the one to give it..." She broke off as she saw her husband re-enter the room. Her questioning glance posed her question much more loudly she ever could have.

The tall, sandy-haired guy dropped back into his seat and favored both the ladies with a broad smile. "Problems solved."

"That easily?" Rebekka couldn't believe that any problem so big could be resolved in mere minutes.

"Two phone calls. That's all it took. Aunt Annetta says there's plenty of room in that newest barn for what you have in the trailer, as well as what's in your storage unit. Everything will be safe and dry there."

"But how will we empty the storage unit? Remember, I'm teaching that day and can't leave campus before three-thirty."

"Handled. Two of the guys from the Sunday School class will do it for you, and you don't have to lift a finger."

"I knew you'd mentioned the Sunday School class, but I didn't realize you were serious. After all, they barely know me."

"Doesn't matter. It's what we do." He extended his hand, palm out and up. "Charles Montgomery and Bill Oates are both self-employed and can set their own schedules. They'll head to Atlanta first thing Friday, rent a truck, empty your unit and even turn in the key if necessary." He was positively beaming. "If all goes as planned, you can leave school and come to *High Lonesome* to supervise the unloading."

"And I've got a great idea," Patti interjected. "When the cottage is ready, we can throw a big social for the whole class, and call it a moving party."

"You want to invite your Sunday School class to my house for a party, and ask them to lift and tote and move me in?"

"Wouldn't be the first time, would it, Patti?"

"Bruce is right," she explained. "Our class can make most

146

anything an excuse for fellowship and good food."

The same objection kept looping through her head, and finally Rebekka said, "But I don't really know all these people. I'd feel funny, if not downright obligated to them, if I let them do all this moving."

"Look, Rebekka," Bruce said, and she noticed that his voice had taken on a more serious tone. "These people want to get to know you, to be your friends, too. And we'd really like to have you become a full-time part of our class."

"That's part of what I mean by obligated," she said, unable to look him in the eye.

"It's called ministry, Rebekka. We'd like for you to join us, but we're going to move you and help you, whether you ever darken the door of our Sunday School room again or not." He grinned at her. "Understand?"

"Seriously," Patti said, "we hope you will become a part of our class, but that's a decision you have to make. We're going to invite you and make you feel as welcome as we can, but ultimately, it's up to you."

"I don't know, guys. I just feel so conflicted."

Patti reached for one of her hands, before she said, "You're welcome to tell me that this is none of our business, but may I ask you why you're so soured on church and God?" She hesitated, then said, "Are you angry with God for Darryl's death?"

At the look of pain that crossed Rebekka's face, Patti hastened to say, "I'm sorry, my friend. I've obviously ripped off a scab that wasn't ready to be removed." She rose and moved around the table, where she leaned in to hug Rebekka. "Please forgive me, and we won't talk about this again."

"Patti's right, we didn't mean to pry. But the guys are still going to move you next Friday, whether we have a moving party later or not. You'll be out of the trailer and the storage unit by the end of the day just like you need to be. Now all you need to do is decide where you're going to stay temporarily."

Rebekka fought back tears that were coming on gangbusters, and had to force herself to look away, lest she lose control. As she glanced about the comfortable kitchen and den combination, she couldn't help but see evidence of the goodness of these two people everywhere she looked. They weren't being nosy, but they were being concerned. And sincere. Perhaps that was what kept her most off-guard, the sincerity with which they approached everything.

Perhaps all churches weren't like the one she'd depended on in Atlanta that had let her down when she needed its ministry most? Certainly it didn't appear that either Patti or Bruce were anything but dependable.

"Why don't we adjourn to the sofas where we can be more comfortable, and you can tell us all about your plans for the cottage," Bruce suggested, and rose to pull out the ladies' chairs.

"Don't forget our surprise," Patti reminded him.

"Ah, yes, the surprise. You two get comfortable, and I'll go get it."

"I can't wait for you to see it," Patti gushed as they took their seats.

"You've really got my curiosity up, you know?"

"That much the better," Patti replied.

Just then Bruce returned carrying a very large, flat object wrapped in heavy brown paper. He set it down on the low table in front of the sofas, looked at Rebekka and said, "This is for your new house."

Rebekka was shell-shocked and couldn't immediately find her tongue. Finally she warbled, her voice sounding like she had a mouth full of marbles. "Can I open it now?"

"If you don't, I'm going to open it," Patti said, as she reached for the hidden treasure. "I can't wait for you to see it."

At that moment, embarrassment and a feeling of unworthiness aside, Rebekka realized that she, too, really wanted to know what was under that brown paper. She reached for the corner and pulled, and was immediately rewarded with the sound of ripping paper. Through the jagged tear in the wrapping, she glimpsed something of many vivid colors, and was inspired to continue freeing whatever it was inside. Then the paper fell away, and she was rewarded with an artist's palette of shape and shadow and brilliant hues of all the primary colors.

"Oh, guys... this is so beautiful. But you shouldn't have, I mean, you really shouldn't have. But I love it. And I love you both."

"Bruce stumbled on it while he was in Atlanta the other day. He took a picture with his phone and sent it to me. We thought it would be a perfect addition to your new cottage."

"It's a print of an Andrew Wyeth original," he explained. But all Rebekka could see was the homey room in a country cottage, much like the little house that would soon be her home. She realized that if her new home was even half as inviting as that room in the painting, she would be beyond happy there.

"I can't wait to try this over the fireplace in the living room," she told her friends.

"That's where we pictured it, too," Bruce said.

"But we didn't want to force our opinion on you. Hang it wherever you'll enjoy it."

Rebekka found it impossible to remove her hand from the gift, almost as if she feared it might disappear into thin air. But she also knew she owed her friends a gesture of appreciation. With much fear, she stood and offered a hug first to Patti, and then to Bruce.

"Hey, guys, whenever I look at this painting, not only will I see the beauty the artist painted into the picture, but I'll see two of the best friends I will ever have." She stood on tiptoe to kiss both of them. "Thank you. Not just for this picture, but for everything you've done for me, for Aimee and me," she corrected herself. "I've never had better friends."

"And if you'd like to leave it here, until you're ready to hang it, that's no problem," Patti said.

As they sat back down, Bruce remarked, "Friendship is a two-way street. You aren't too shabby a friend yourself, you know?"

His words startled her, and Rebekka fought back the quick retort that fought her tongue to get life. She also considered what he'd said.

"You want to tell me how I've been a good a friend to you as you both have been to me? All I can see is you all doing so much, and I'm not doing anything in return."

Bruce looked at Patti. "You want to take this one?' To Rebekka he said, "My wife is the more eloquent one. All I got was a pretty face."

Despite her efforts otherwise, Rebekka couldn't stifle the laughter that escaped her. Patti and then Bruce quickly joined her. When the moment of hysteria had passed, Patti said, "Bruce got more than looks, I promise you. He also got the gift of blarney, and I wouldn't have him any other way."

As she observed the interaction between them, she found herself both awed and envious of her two friends, who were obviously so comfortable with themselves. At that moment, she missed Darryl with a crippling ache in her gut that hadn't been there for a while.

Does it ever completely go away?

"To answer your question, Rebekka, I'd put it like this. You've heard the Scripture that talks about it's more blessed to give than to receive."

Rebekka nodded, uncertain where her friend was going.

"When you allow us to help you, you make it possible for us to feel blessed. And we thank you for that."

"But I don't have any way to do for you everything you've done for me. Starting with just basic friendship and welcome from almost the first moment I arrived in town."

"Payback isn't the issue," Bruce said, before Rebekka could continue. "At least not payback to us."

"I don't understand."

"Some day," Patti said quietly, "when you're more on your feet than you are now, you will give of yourself and your blessings to someone else, but without expectation of repayment."

"I don't know if I totally follow you. How will I know of needs?"

"You may not always know of a need," Bruce interjected. "There's a Realtor in town who has made millions here. The other day, because I happened to be behind his car in the drive through at one of the fast food places at breakfast, I got my breakfast free. Now I wasn't needy, but who can't use a few more dollars?"

"I still don't understand?"

"When Mr. Mac paid for his food, he left four one hundred dollar bills with the lady at the to-go checkout, with instructions to use it to pay for each order behind him, as long as the money held out. If I hadn't known who was ahead of me, I wouldn't have had a clue. But those people behind me didn't know."

"So you're saying he did a general good deed, instead of meeting a specific need?"

"Exactly. Can you imagine how you'd feel if you pulled up to the window with your money ready, and the clerk tells you that someone ahead of you has already paid for your food? It's not the dollar amount, it's the generosity and the surprise that speaks to you."

Rebekka had to admit she'd feel pretty blessed.

"But not half as blessed as Mr. Mac feels," Patti said. "And he often anonymously underwrites specific needs as well. More than one child is enrolled in pre-school because Mr. Mac quietly wrote a check. And that's all I'm going to say on that."

"But you wouldn't have to underwrite pre-school tuition, or leave four hundred dollars at the drive-through," Bruce explained. "You could leave a ten dollar bill and give the clerk the same instructions. The concept is to keep your eyes and ears open to determine where and how you can give without getting anything tangible back in return."

As she pondered all she'd heard, she realized that her friends were on to something. "I get it," she said finally. "I repay you by doing for someone else, and we all get to feel blessed in the process."

"By jove," Bruce said, "I believe she's got it, Patti old girl."

She couldn't help but laugh at her friend's very bad British impersonation, but she also knew that behind the charade was a very genuine man, with a heart as big as the all outdoors. She realized something else, as well. If anyone in Cedar Mountain deserved an explanation for her bad attitude about church, it was Patti and Bruce Martin.

"Hey, guys. You asked me why I was so soured on church and God. I'd like to tell you. Here. Now."

"That's not necessary," Patti replied. "I was out of line to ask, and I should be asking your forgiveness."

"But you see," Rebekka said, "you were exactly right. I am soured on everything to do with God, but it has less to do with losing Darryl than it does with how I was treated by people who I thought were my friends from church."

"We're here to listen," Bruce assured her. "But only if you want to share. It's your call."

Rebekka knew if she didn't forge ahead while she had her courage corralled, she might never tell this story.

"It's like this," she said. By the time she'd finished almost twenty minutes later, she had explained the relationship that had existed between her and her mother-in-law from the moment they met. Patti and Bruce understood Judith's standing in the church, and the financial clout she wielded. Rebekka shared about various church members who had pledged to stand with her and Aimee, but had skittered like water bugs when the lights go on, once Judith began applying coercion.

"So you're telling us that Darryl's mother used her money to persuade people not to help you and Aimee? And she didn't contribute one dime to Darryl's funeral?"

"That's about the size of it," Rebekka confirmed. "When the Sunday School class we'd been a part of since our marriage pledged to cover our rent for six months, Judith quietly let it be known that if they did, she would pull her pledge of support for the class's main mission outreach project. Without her money, the project would have been sidelined. So suddenly I get a call that because of 'circumstances,' they're not going to be able to help us after all."

"How low and dirty," was all Bruce could say.

"Definitely un-Christian in several ways," Patti said.

"It took a while for me to catch on, but after several offers of assistance suddenly vanished into thin air, I began to see the fingerprints. It was always Judith." She hesitated. "What's more, people suddenly began to shun us. I realize now it was because they were embarrassed, but in the beginning, all I could see was one after another turning their backs on us when we needed them most."

She stopped and examined her hands, before continuing. "Finally, Aimee and I just gave up church, although she begged to go. And when we moved here, I guess I figured this church would be just like the one we left." She made a nervous wave with her hands.

"Although I know now that makes no sense whatsoever."

"Our church isn't perfect," Bruce said, "because we're all humans, but I think if you'll give us a chance, we can show you a different picture from what you saw in Atlanta."

"Just think about it, honey. No pressure," Patti said.

They dropped the subject and Rebekka and Aimee were soon headed home. After all, church was the next morning, and for a change, she was hungry to go and fellowship with people who wanted to be her new friends. As she was getting ready for bed, that evening's conversation echoed in her head. "Our church isn't perfect," Bruce had said. "Just think about it," Patti had encouraged.

As she slipped into rest, she heard herself saying, "I will think about it, guys."

CHAPTER SEVEN

MISPLACED GRATITUDE

T he next week was a blur. Sunday at church, Rebekka had been surprised to see how her change of attitude and new vision made the experience all the more real and pertinent. Her heart felt warmed. In Sunday School, Charles and Bill had assured her that it was their pleasure to help, and had waved away any offer of payment.

"But you've got truck rental and gasoline, not to mention your time."

"It's all covered, Rebekka. You don't owe us anything."

She decided to stop pressing the issue. "God bless you both," she said at last, as she gave each guy a gentle hug and felt nonetheless uncomfortable for doing so.

"He's already blessed us both, immensely," Charles said. "Trust me."

I can literally see the good feeling these guys have as a result of helping me. That's what I need.

Getting back into the groove in school on Monday morning was a challenge for both her and Aimee, and when the dismissal bell rang that afternoon, Rebekka sent a silent prayer of thanksgiving heavenward. It had been a very long day.

She had elected to stay at the trailer until the end of the week, but had informed Aunt Annetta that she and Aimee would be staying at *High Lonesome* on Friday night. That last day of the week, which was also the last day of the month, promised to be a day to remember. She would be vacating the trailer and turning the key over to Mr. Barton. No love lost there, for certain. Her furniture would be coming from storage, and that alone promised to be a family reunion. She and Aimee would be moving into the big house with Aunt Annetta until the cottage was ready.

Friday was also payday, which meant a new infusion of cash would appear in her account, and it was the day she would make the first payment to Mr. Goddard on the car repair. Thanks to the anonymous guardian angel who had paid off Darryl's funeral, she would be able to make more than the minimum payment on the car.

All in all, it promised to be a good week, one she was eagerly anticipating. It still bugged her that she couldn't identify who had paid the mortuary, but she prayed that they were as blessed by their generosity as she had been. Even if that someone was her mother-in-law, although the pragmatist on her left shoulder demanded to know if she'd lost her mind to even consider Judith capable of such generosity.

That Friday, she was as antsy as her students for the end of the day to come. While she tried to concentrate on teaching, when she least expected she found her mind wandering to Charles and Bill. Where were they? Did they have any trouble getting a truck? The guy at the storage unit could be difficult when he wanted to be. Even though she'd called and given the guys clearance to get her furniture, had the old curmudgeon given them grief? She'd given them her cell number. Surely if they'd had problems, they would have called.

Finally, when she could stand it no longer, the afternoon bell rang, and the students piled out anxious for their weekend to begin.

Better get out of my way, guys. This is one teacher who will mow you down today. I've got things to do!

Knowing it would earn her a reprimand if the principal found out, she made her way to the office and signed out fifteen minutes early. Teachers were supposed to remain in their classrooms for thirty minutes after the last class, in case students needed to drop by for help. But as she well knew, today of all days, there would be no one wanting help. The campus was already deserted and she had other matters to attend.

At the bank, she verified her payroll deposit, pulled out some cash to go "on the hip" as her father would have said, and headed to the garage with checkbook in hand. She'd already written the check for two hundred more than the set amount, and was feeling pretty good about herself.

The garage appeared in the distance, and she unconsciously speeded up, never having been so anxious or excited about paying a bill.

"I'm sorry, Mrs. Austin," the mechanic said after he'd wiped his greasy hands on a gasoline-soaked rag. "But it's been paid."

When she had held out his check, instead of taking it, the mechanic had almost backed away. "Your bill's been paid in full," he'd said. You don't owe me anything, but I hope you'll bring your business back to me next time."

"But Mr. Goddard," she'd protested. "There's no way somebody paid my bill. It can't be."

Could it? This was like déjà vu at the funeral home all over again.

"Can you tell me who it was?"

"A man. Stranger. Never seen him before. Wearing a nice suit, too. I was afraid the whole time he was here he was going to get himself greasy."

As she glanced around the garage, where all manner of cars and car parts rested in no semblance of order, Rebekka had to admit that whoever the stranger was, he'd had ample opportunity to ruin his suit. And while her slacks and top weren't designer fashion, she nevertheless looked more carefully at her own clothes and their proximity to the grime.

"This makes absolutely no sense."

"I'm sorry, Mrs. Austin. I just figured he was your daddy, come to do a good deed for his daughter, and I took his money. I figured either you knew, or he would tell you."

"I'm more than happy that you've gotten your money, and I appreciate that you worked with me on this bill, but I have not the first clue who paid it."

"You're not mad at me, are you?" the mechanic asked.

"Most certainly not," Rebekka assured him. "I just wish I had some clue who my angel is."

Mr. Goddard said, "Well, I can't tell you who he is, but I'll bet I can show you his picture."

His picture?

He motioned for her to follow, and being careful not to brush up against the grease that seemed to be the glue holding the garage together, she joined him in the small office area.

"A man can't be too careful, you know." He was fumbling with a device that Rebekka thought resembled a VCR. "I've got a security camera aimed at this desk, so if anybody tries to rob me, if they don't leave here dead, at least I can show police what they looked like."

A picture? Savvy.

He turned to his paid bill file, thumbed through it, and said.

"He paid this on November 19. He punched buttons on the security unit. "Ah, here we are. Now it was about four o'clock in the afternoon. I remember, because I had a doctor's appointment at two o'clock." He gave her a look that reminded Rebekka of an owl, peering down at its prey. "Ain't it awful how the doctors think a person can just hang up the closed sign on their business and go sit for an hour?"

Rebekka agreed that it was, although silently, she was screaming for him to find the picture.

"So I'd been back about ten minutes when the feller come. So let's go back to three-thirty and move forward."

She watched over his shoulders, as he ran the images slide-show style across the computer screen. Unfortunately, everything was moving so fast, all she could see was a blur. She hoped he could see better than she could. He stopped the flow, backed it up, then moved forward again and stopped.

"There he is," the old man announced. "That's him. I'd know him anywhere." Mr. Goddard got up from the computer and indicated that Rebekka should sit. For once, she didn't worry about her clothes, but quickly sat down. What met her eyes was the face of a man she estimated to be around fifty years old. Blond hair, kind of long in the back. Any other distinguishing features were too small to see on the security photo. He looked like a lawyer, but all in all, an ordinary looking lawyer.

"Now I remember about him." The mechanic snapped his fingers. "The scar. This feller had a little scar on his right cheek, kinda like a question mark."

After quizzing him further, Rebekka knew she had other stops to make. There were still a few boxes in the trailer to load, and Mr. Barton had indicated he would be there at five o'clock to collect his key and take possession of the trailer. She would surrender the little home on wheels without a fuss, but the identity of the man with the money and the scar troubled her more.

Obviously, the money wasn't from him. First the funeral home and now the garage. He was just the messenger. More importantly was who he represented. And why? Rebekka feared until she could answer those questions, she wouldn't be any closer to the answers. What bothered her most was the possibility that someone was spying on her. Watching her every move. Stalking her, even. While payment of those two debts was a godsend, the circumstances around them made her almost want to look a gift horse in the mouth.

True to his word, at five o'clock on the dot, Mr. Barton's old pickup truck pulled into the drive. Rebekka was coming out the door with the last of the boxes in her arms. All that remained was a final walk-through to assure she hadn't overlooked anything. One thing for certain, it felt like she was moving out with more than she'd brought with her.

How did I manage to acquire so much in the short time I've lived here? I haven't had enough extra money to go on shopping binges.

"You 'bout out of here, Mrs. Austin? It's after five o'clock, you know." The landlord stood in the living room, his back to the wall, and his arms crossed over his chest. He could be the poster boy for uncooperative, she thought.

She shot a look at the clock over the stove. Five-oh-two, it read. "Just about, Mr. Barton. I just need to take one more look around." Deciding she was tired of his overbearing ways, she said, "You know, Mr. Barton, by law my rent actually runs through midnight tonight."

"You're crazy, missy, if you think I'm coming back at midnight to conclude this matter." The older gentleman was positively sputtering, and Rebekka feared he might have a stroke.

"Nor am I coming back at that hour, either, Mr. Barton. So if you'll just work with me for two or three more minutes, we can both be on the way to our respective destinations." *And I won't have to deal with your unpleasant attitude any more, either!*

She made one quick sweep through the trailer, opening closet doors and cabinets, being sure to shut them as she moved on. Finally, convinced she'd done all she could, she met the landlord at the door and handed him his key.

"I'm out of here, Mr. Barton. I hope you have a very nice evening." She really wanted to say much more than that, but decided there was no value in venting her frustration at that late date. The time to have stood up for herself had been weeks before. But then that was something she wasn't totally comfortable doing. She mentally scratched her head for a moment. But perhaps it was a skill she needed to perfect. Starting with her mother-in-law.

"So when should I expect my security deposit refund?"

"Like I told you, the law says I don't have to write it 'til thirty days after you vacate. So you can expect the check to be cut by

December 30."

"I'll also expect it to be for the full amount I posted, too. There were things wrong here when I moved in that you still haven't fixed. And I paid the rent on time each month. Don't think you're gonna stick me with the tab for that maintenance.

"You sure do know how to be bossy, don't you?"

"If you call standing up for myself being bossy, then I guess I'm bossy. Good night, Mr. Barton." *And I'm gonna keep on being bossy, too.*

Just the thought a few minutes earlier of Darryl's mother sent cold chills cascading down her spine. Judith? Surely not; it couldn't be. There was no way Judith could be her secret benefactor. Not that she didn't have the money, but the Judith she knew would have paid those bills in such a way that the entire world would have known. Rebekka's nose would have been rubbed in it in the process.

Still…

Upon her arrival at *High Lonesome,* she resisted all temptation and drove right on by the cottage up to the main house. More specifically to the barn behind the house, where her other possessions from the trailer had already been deposited. While she was unloading the last of the items from her car, the rental truck from Atlanta with Charles Montgomery behind the wheel pulled in and backed up toward the large door opening. Immediately behind him, driving the truck they'd used to go to Atlanta, was Bill who jumped out to guide the truck driver.

In the excitement of seeing her possessions again, Rebekka forgot all about the question of who was paying her bills, and began to enjoy seeing pieces that had suddenly became more precious as they came off the truck. It wasn't long before the truck was empty, the barn was pushing close to full, and she was aching to see all of that furniture in place in the cottage. She already knew where each piece would go. She'd planned it out in her mind during the long nights of the past week.

By the time she'd thanked the guys and promised them a special thank you over Christmas, it was time to join Aimee in the house where she'd been since Patti dropped her there earlier in the evening. Dinner was homemade chicken pot pies and fresh apple turnovers around the fire in the den. After relaxing and just enjoying the fellowship with their hostess who had, by this point, become such a loved and precious friend, Rebekka and Aimee excused themselves and made their way upstairs.

Fortunately, the next day was Saturday. School and its hectic morning routine that would have to be altered, would come soon enough. Once Aimee was read to and tucked into her new but temporary bed, Rebekka retired to her own bed. Despite her protests that the two of them could share one bed for the few nights they would be there, Aunt Annette had insisted. Instead, they were sleeping in a two-room suite, with a connecting door between the two rooms. Rebekka had left the door open in case Aimee woke up in the night, and became frightened because she was in a new place.

She turned out the light, but before she could turn off her mind, the matter of who had paid something over two thousand dollars to satisfy her debts came back front and center. The question

THREE GIFTS FOR CHRISTMAS

would, she knew, keep her awake for hours if she didn't address it. *So I'll address it!*

So few people knew about the car repair costs, and even fewer knew about the outstanding funeral bill. In each instance, she could count those people on the fingers of one hand. Patti and Bruce were generous, but she didn't see them dropping that kind of money, especially not right here at Christmas. Aunt Annetta knew some of the story, but not enough for her to put two and two together. All she knew were generalities. And Darryl's police buddies had claimed they knew nothing about the balance owing on their friend's service. For sure there was no way they could have known about the car repairs.

Which left Judith.

Again, the possibility that her former mother-in-law had spies on the ground in Cedar Mountain reporting ever move she made, everything she did, was unsettling. In addition to reporting her activities, might they also have been poisoning the town about her? The possibility was paralyzing? Could Judith also have been the mysterious buyer of the trailer, the person who had insisted that she had to move?

The enormity of all she was thinking was more than Rebekka could handle, and she jumped from the bed and began to pace. Could her mother-in-law actually be guilty of such deceit and subversive actions? But who else could it be? As she allowed the facts as she knew them to flow in front of her mind's eye, the answer became more definitive. There could only be one conclusion.

Judith Austin was the guilty party. There could be no doubt about it. The question was... WHY? Now, knowing what she knew, what was Rebekka going to do? Did she just ignore everything, give silent thanks, and go on? While part of her endorsed that course of action, there was a more pragmatic side that argued since Judith had successfully gotten away with what she'd done so far, when would she stop? Where would she stop? When would Judith's next act of generosity bite Rebekka on the behind?

It's a scary feeling having someone you can't even see messing in your life, especially when you don't know where she'll strike next!

She finally crawled back under the covers, as much for warmth as anything. But sleep was long coming, and morning dawned before she was even close to ready. Unfortunately, when her feet hit the cold floor, she was immediately transported back to her dilemma. If Judith was the responsible party, how should she respond?

Her original plan had been to spend a part of the day at the cottage, just looking and thinking and planning and trying to get as close to her new home as she could. Over breakfast, she made the decision that pleasures of the heart would have to wait while she dealt with business of the head. Otherwise, she would never get a minute's peace.

Breakfast over, beds made, showers taken, and a couple of phone calls made, she and Aimee were soon headed into town. Patti had welcomed them, saying that Merry Beth would be thrilled to have her best friend come to play.

When the girls were settled in the basement, far enough way

they couldn't overhear, Rebekka quickly brought her friend up to speed. First the deal with the funeral bill, and now the car repair as well.

"I know it's not you and Bruce," she'd stated flat out, hoping to catch a glimpse of confirmation on her friend's face.

"It's not that we wouldn't do it," Patti said quietly. "But right now, with Bruce trying to get the office open here in Cedar Mountain, we just wouldn't have it to spare."

Rebekka leaned to hug her friend. "And I wouldn't want you to spend that kind of money on me. Just knowing that you would if you could, means everything." She sat up, cleared her throat and became all business again. "So it's not you, it's not Aunt Annetta, it's not Darryl's friends on the force."

"So what are you saying?"

"Judith. Darryl's mother. Who else could it be?"

Patti's expression was pained and questioning, but she said nothing.

"Don't you see? She's got spies here in town. They probably know I'm here right now and are reporting to her."

Patti said nothing for a few seconds. "Girlfriend, you been watching too many of those TV mysteries you love." She chuckled. "Spies? Here in Cedar Mountain? Who? How? You're the last newcomer to move here in the last few months."

Rebekka didn't want to think badly of her friend for bursting her balloon, but at the same time, Patti was making some valid points.

"It might not be her," she said at last. Her pleading expression spoke louder than any words she might manufacture. "But if not her. Who? Just tell me that? Because this is going to drive me crazy."

Patti got up, checked on the girls and came back into the kitchen. "I'm going to fix us each a cup of Russian Tea, and then we're going to take this thing apart and examine every piece."

"I'm not chained to my theory," Rebekka confessed, and realized that she almost hoped it was someone besides Judith. The prospect of having to feel grateful to the old witch after all the agony she'd endured at the woman's hands was enough to make her want to throw up. "If you can find another likely candidate for sainthood, lay it on me." She grimaced. "'Cause St. Judith does absolutely nothing for me."

When they were settled back on the den couch with their steaming cups of fragrant tea and spices, Patti sat her cup down and reached into a drawer in the large table in front of them. Pulling out a yellow legal pad and pen, she said, "Just bear with me here for a few minutes. I want to get everything down on paper so we can examine it. Separately and together."

"Whatever works for you works for me." Rebekka sat quietly, while her friend's pen made scratches across the page, speaking only when Patti stopped writing to ask a question. When she finished, Patti scratched her head with the pen, and said, "It makes absolutely no sense that Judith is your man... er, guardian angel. But yet I can't see it being anyone else, either." She dropped the pen and ran through her hair with both hands. "This is maddening, Rebekka."

"It is maddening," she agreed. "And do you know what I think I should do?"

"From the look on your face, I'm almost afraid to guess. But I sure hope it's not what I think it is."

"I'm going to have to confront the woman. Once and for all. Get it out on the table and go from there."

"That's what I was afraid you were going to say." She turned so that they were looking each other in the eye. "When you say confront, do you mean like drive to Atlanta and visit her on her turf?"

Rebekka considered her friend's words. The prospect of bearding the lioness as she had begun to consider Judith in her den wasn't a comfortable proposition. Besides, she would have to spend time and gas money driving to Atlanta.

"I'll call her," she said at last. "I'll call her, I'll put her on speaker phone, and you'll be with me to listen in."

"Hey, friend. Hold up a second. You know by law you're supposed to tell her she's on speaker? How do you think that would go over?"

"Like I didn't trust her."

"So?"

"I don't trust her. That's why I want you as a witness." She halted, and decided to go for broke, because she'd suddenly understood why it was so critical to know whether Judith was the benefactor. "If Judith paid those two bills, sooner or later, there's going to be a payment demand from her that will cost me much more than two thousand dollars." She stopped, realizing the severity of her charge. "Unfortunately, I know that woman too well. What I can tell you without hesitation is that she doesn't like me even one little bit."

As she spoke, incident after incident in the past, beginning before she and Darryl had even been engaged, came flooding back. Much to her regret right at that moment, she'd never confided in her boyfriend and later her husband, all the dastardly, underhanded, even cruel deeds his mother had perpetrated on her and on them.

That's where I made my mistake. I should have stood up to her, and I should have exposed her to Darryl for exactly what she is. A vengeful woman so full of hate the only reason she eats is to aggravate her stomach.

Those last words had been her daddy's favorite phrase to describe someone soured on the world and everyone in it. Right at that moment, she missed her daddy, more than she had in a long time. How wonderful it would have been to have spilled all her concerns to him, and heard him say, "Don't fret, sugar. I'll take care of it."

If Rebekka wanted the matter settled, she would have to do it herself.

"No, I won't waste my time driving to Atlanta. But I am going to call her."

"When? How? You don't have a home right now, remember?"

Rebekka thought quickly. "Will Bruce be where he can watch the girls for an hour or so after lunch?"

Patti grabbed her phone. I'll just find out." Rebekka waited while the couple handled business. "He says he'll be home by two o'clock, and he can give us two hours."

"Great!"

"You still haven't told me where we're going to make this call from. We can't do it here."

"We'll go to barn at *High Lonesome* where all my furniture's stored. We ought to have privacy there."

It was agreed that Rebekka would return to the country, leaving Aimee to play. Patti would come out as soon as Bruce relieved her, and they would tell Aunt Annetta they were going to the barn to look at different pieces to decide where to place them in the cottage.

"She'll buy that," Patti agreed. "Only I don't think I've ever once deceived my aunt."

Rebekka felt a momentary pang of guilt that she was making her friend feel uncomfortable."

"Why can't we just tell Aunt Annetta everything? She'll understand. Then we can just go upstairs to your bedroom and make the call. None of this slipping around?"

In truth, Rebekka didn't like the underhanded tone of what she was proposing any more than Patti did. At one point, she asked herself if she wasn't being equally as guilty as Judith was. But in the end, she reasoned, she wasn't comfortable confiding in Patti's aunt, although she couldn't have explained why.

"I wish we could," she said at last. "But I think we have to do it this way." She regarded her friend with a critical eye. "I won't force you to be a part of this, if you truly don't want to. But I still need you to keep Aimee, because I am going to call."

After a space of time that felt hours if not days long, Patti said. "I'll be at *High Lonesome* by two-thirty. But please tell Aunt Annetta your story before I get there, and be in the barn before me. That way I don't have to be in on the deception."

Am I really as twisted and evil as Judith? The prospect that they could be identical personalities was both unsettling and down-right scary. Yet that's what I'm hearing Patti imply.

She left both troubled but resolute.

Following lunch of soup and sandwiches, she said, "I'm going down to the barn to look at all my furniture. Patti's coming out, and we're going to try to make some decisions on where certain pieces need to go."

"I'd be glad to help if you need me," her aunt said as she patted her mouth with her napkin and rose from her chair. The smile she favored Rebekka with was, Rebekka thought, one thousand megawatts bright.

Caught! This is what you get for being less than honest. Finally she said, "It's probably pretty chilly down there. You'd be more comfortable here by the fire." Then inspiration prompted her guilty conscience. "Patti will come back to the house with me afterwards, and we can tell you everything. Besides, we may be running back and forth to the cottage."

The older woman crossed the room and laid her hand on Rebekka's arm. "I understand my dear. You are so very anxious to get into your own place. I do hope we can make that happen by this time next week."

Feeling far beyond low and dirty, Rebekka made her way across the back yard to the barn that held all her worldly possessions. So if everything was here, why did she feel so displaced?

When Patti arrived, Rebekka wasted little time getting down to business. After locking the walk-through door to make it more difficult for anyone to intrude, she pulled up two dining chairs next to an end table, switched her phone to speaker mode, and punched in the number she'd once sworn never to remember. Only she had. That was just one indication of the hold Judith still had on her.

"Hello?"

"Hello, Judith."

"Who is this? Tell me this instance or I'll hang up."

"It's Rebekka, Judith."

"Rebekka who?"

She saw Patti's eyebrows shoot up, and the two friends exchanged glances that were pregnant with question and shock.

"Rebekka. Darryl's wife?"

"Oh. You? What do you want? And how did you get my number?"

"It's the same number you've had since I first met you," she said, feeling like more than just a simpleton. This woman really had the ability to bring out the little child in her.

"So why are you bothering me?"

"Did you have a good Thanksgiving, Judith?"

There was a long silence, before a voice edged with venom said, "Darryl wasn't here. What do you think?"

"Aimee and I missed him, too." In reality, she realized, she'd actually enjoyed the holiday, although there had been moments when Darryl's absence had been overwhelming. *Should I feel guilty?*

"You didn't miss him half as bad as I did," Judith bit back. "You had your child, I didn't."

Rebekka wanted to fire back that Judith could have had her grandchild if she'd wanted, but she knew that no good would come of the charge, so she bit her lip and said instead, "I'm sorry you had a bad Thanksgiving."

"So is that all you called for, to ask me how my Thanksgiving was? If so, I guess we're through."

Fearful she was about to hear the other end of an empty line, Rebekka freaked. "Wait, Judith. There is something else."

"Well spit it out. I've got things to do."

She glanced across at Patti, and realized that despite the chilly temperatures in the barn, beads of sweat that felt the size of large grapes had broken out all over her body. Her friend's eyes telegraphed encouragement and support.

"Listen Judith, I called to thank you."

"To thank me! My gosh, whatever for? I did so much for the both of you, and not once, ever, have you told me thank you. So I can't imagine why you would want to say those words now?"

For one thing, I've told you thank you many, many times. You just didn't want to hear it. And much of what you're claiming to have done was actually interference on a grand scale.

But she recognized the futility of any rebuttals. Better to say what she called to say and get off the phone. Judith would obviously be happy, and she knew she would.

"I wanted to thank you for stepping in to pay the balance of Darryl's funeral service and for paying my car repair bill."

"You want to thank me for what?"

"I know he was probably your attorney or someone from his

179

office, but both places described the same man who came in with cash to pay both of those bills."

"And you think I paid them?" the voice on the other end said at last.

"It had to be you, Judith. No one else knew about the bills. So I just wanted to let you know that Aimee and I appreciate it."

Rebekka couldn't decide if the reaction on the other end was tears or laughter or snorts of derision.

"Let me make one thing abundantly clear to you, Missy! I neither knew about your low-account debts that you've been trying to beat. Nor would I have paid one red cent on anything that might benefit you or that illegitimate child of yours!"

Illegitimate child! Aimee?

Fire shot up Rebekka's back, and any plans she had to play nice flew straight out the window. "Think of me what you will, Judith, but you will not slander mine and Darryl's daughter, and your only grandchild with the label illegitimate."

"Darryl had the mumps when he was a teenager. They told him he would never be able to father children. And then you come up pregnant!" There was a heavy pause, before the tirade continued. "You may have fooled my son, but you will never fool me!"

"Yes, Darryl had the mumps. And the doctor told him he MIGHT never be able to have children. They didn't tell him absolutely not."

"I just know what I know. I begged Darryl to leave you after you got pregnant, but he was so wrapped up in your devious ways, he always insisted the baby was his. But I knew better."

Rebekka found herself unable to contain the words she had wanted to say for so long.

"I'm finally glad to know what the burr under your saddle has been. And I'm sorry you choose to believe as you do. The only one who's hurting and missing out is you, Judith. Aimee could be a comfort to you, just like she is to me. But if you choose to believe that Darryl isn't her father, there's nothing I can do about it."

"She could take a paternity test!"

The words were out there before Rebekka was ready to hear them. And while her knee-jerk reaction was to agree to the woman's demands, the more pragmatic side of her nature took over. "You would believe the words of a blood test over the word of your son, Judith?"

"Then I could know for sure."

"And what would you do if you knew for sure?"

"I'd make sure the little girl has all the things that you'll never be able to give her." She hesitated. "You know, if you'd worked and helped Darryl, you all wouldn't have had any money problems."

Knowing she was flogging a dead horse, Rebekka said, "Darryl and I decided together, Judith, that I wouldn't go back to work until Aimee was in kindergarten. That was our decision."

"Yeah, he said that, too. But I never believed him. He always sang your praises. You had him buffaloed. I'll always hate you for that."

"Yes, Judith, I imagine you will. It's been nice talking to you." *But let's don't do it again sometime!*

"Wait. I have to know if Aimee is Darryl's child." Rebekka thought she detected the hint of a sob. "I just have to know, Rebekka. Otherwise, I'll die always wondering."

"You do know, Judith. Your son told you that Aimee is his. If his word is good enough for me, it should be good enough for you, too!"

"But you don't...."

"Goodbye, Judith."

Rebekka hit the disconnect key.

"Well, I guess that answers that and a whole lot more."

CHAPTER EIGHT

BEGINNING TO LOOK LIKE CHRISTMAS

R ebekka sat for the longest saying nothing. There was so much that she wanted to say, but somehow, the words wouldn't get themselves in sync and come out in an orderly fashion.

"I never saw that one coming." She cradled her head in her arms, almost as if it had suddenly grown too heavy to maintain its own balance. "That explains everything." She favored her friend with a knowing stare. "I mean everything."

"You never guessed this was her problem?"

Rebekka rose from the hard dining chair and moved over to a chest that had belonged to her mother's mother. Fingering the

185

richness of the burled walnut top, and getting from it a quick trip back to another time and another place where insanity didn't run rampant, she said. "Not only that, Darryl evidently didn't take her seriously when she tried to poison his mind against me."

Patti had walked over to join her. "And he figured he'd always be there to run interference, so there was no need to burden you with knowing your mother-in-law believed you'd been unfaithful to her son."

She opened a drawer, looking for what she didn't know. "But Darryl was wrong, wasn't he?"

She lay her head down on the top of the antique chest and the tears flowed. There was nothing she could do to staunch them. It was like they had a mind and a will of their own. She was just along for the water-logged ride.

"Oh, Patti," she sobbed. "I miss him so much. I don't think it's hurt this bad since that day, about a week after the funeral, when I woke up and realized that I was a widow with no family, no real friends. Just a small child who was good as gold, but who looked to me for everything. I didn't know if I could deliver. How was I going to take care of me and her?"

"I'm not going to say I know how you felt," Patti said, taking a moment to hug her friend ever so lightly. "I can only imagine how confused and scared you were." She fumbled in her jeans pocket and pulled out a slightly used tissue. "Here. Wipe your tears and clean up your face. If you go back to Aunt Annetta looking like that, you're going to frighten her big time."

Oh my gosh. Aunt Annetta!

"I told her you'd come back to the house with me. She's going to be expecting both of us."

"You can't let her see you looking like that."

"Look, just follow my lead."

Rebekka turned off the lights, locked the walk-through door behind them, and led Patti across the huge back yard to the house. Aunt Annetta was coming down the hall from the den as they came in through the kitchen. One look at Rebekka, and she stopped short. Confusion and concern were tattooed on her normally cheery face.

"Oh, my dear. What's wrong? Are you injured?"

I'm hurt beyond words, but I can't share that pain with this good woman. Not after all she's done for me and Aimee.

"Digging in my furniture and all those things that were so precious to Darryl was a harder stroll down memory lane than I expected. I'm afraid I kind of lost it."

"Totally understandable, my dear." The older woman enveloped Rebekka in a gentle but deliberate hug. "For months after I lost A.J., I'd encounter something from our wonderful life together, and before it was over, I'd be in tears."

"It's rough," Rebekka agreed. "I thought I was over all of this, but I guess I'm not."

"Oh, Rebekka. When you love a man like you loved Darryl and I loved A.J., you never truly get over losing them. The pain gets softer and less bitter, but it never completely leaves you. You just learn to live with it and love it, because it's a mark of how much each of you meant to the other."

Patti was watching Rebekka closely. "We better change the subject, Aunt Annetta, before we get this one on another crying jag."

"Of course, you're exactly right. I'm sorry, my dear." She patted Rebekka on the back. "Why don't you go up to your room and wash your face and join us in the den whenever you're ready?"

It could never be said that Aunt Annetta wasn't a lady through and through. Rebekka excused herself and hurried for the stairs, grateful both for the time to pull herself together, and that Patti would hold down the fort until she got back. It took a few minutes of washing her face, combing her hair and applying a little camouflaging makeup to the point that she felt presentable.

"Did I miss anything?" she asked, as she strolled into the den. "You weren't talking about me, were you?"

Patti exhibited the devlish grin Rebekka had come to cherish. "But of course. You were the main topic of conversation."

"Don't believe her," Aunt Annetta cautioned. "We were talking about Bruce and the girls." She smiled at her niece. "You know, he reminds me so much of your Uncle A.J. That same easy-going spirit. I don't think I ever once asked him to look after Jan, or even the both of you, that he didn't do it. And a couple of times I know for certain he re-arranged his plans to make it happen." She hesitated, and Rebekka was convinced she saw tears in the corners of the older woman's eyes. "Count your many blessings, my dear. You are fortunate."

"I know that, Aunt Annetta. God truly smiled on me when He put Bruce in my life."

She believes God put Bruce in her path. I don't *guess I ever thought that about Darryl, but I can see now that God did exactly that. Oh, God, please be sure Darryl is happy in heaven.* The thought that the man who had treated her like royalty wasn't happy in his eternal home was something she couldn't process.

"So now," their hostess said, "we need to talk about Christmas."

"What about it, Auntie?"

"You girls remember I told you a couple of weeks ago that we were going to have a big Christmas party like we had before we lost Jan and Uncle A.J."

"Are you sure that's wise? Aside from the work, are you emotionally ready to confront such a big reminder of what you've lost?"

Rebekka suddenly saw the woman in the wingback by the fire totally consumed with a glow that she hadn't seen before. There was no obvious explanation for it, but it was definitely there.

"My dears," she regarded each of them with a look that spoke pure love. "I'm more than ready. Merry Beth and Aimee are at that magical age, when Santa Claus comes and they see him and talk with him There's no hurt that scene won't erase. Plus, we have two new members of our family who will join us this year." She paused, then leaned forward, and whispered, "Besides, one of Santa's elves has let it slip that this is going to be a very special Christmas for each and every one of us." There was a twinkle in her eye, Rebekka thought. Or was there?

Convinced they couldn't dissuade her, Rebekka and Patti spent the rest of the visit comparing calendars and notes, finally determining that Saturday night, the twenty-first of December, would be the most opportune time.

"Very good," Aunt Annetta confirmed. The twenty-first, three weeks from tonight, it is."

Patti and Rebekka left, headed to Patti's car. "Thanks, friend, for not giving me away back there."

"Listen. After I heard how your mother-in-law regards both you and Aimee, I can't fault you. Now we're back to square one. If not her? WHO?"

"I've never been more stumped. I confess." She hooked her arm around her friend's elbow. "You know what? I'm just going to accept both those payments as a gesture of good will and pray that whoever is responsible is even half as blessed by their gift as I am by their generosity."

"If anybody deserves this, it's you," Patti said. "It's about time things turned around for you."

"I just wonder what Aunt Annetta's special Christmas surprise is. She's got something up her sleeve. Don't you agree?"

"She does," Patti said. "But it's been so long since I've seen her this animated, until I don't care what's got her excited."

"I guess we'll find out on the twenty-first."

"That's three weeks away."

"You know," Patti said, "it sounds so much longer when you say it."

She pondered the path in front of them, before she said, "I was really dreading this first Christmas without Darryl, but now I think it's gonna be okay. We'll still be family, even if we aren't here together." She hesitated, then swiped back a tear that had run rogue out of her eye. "All I want for Christmas is a family."

Rebekka followed her friend back to town, where, to no one's surprise, Aimee was not ready to leave her friend. No amount of cajoling, promises of other play dates, or even shallow threats would dissuade the child from her determination to stay at the Martin household. Rebekka hesitated to grab her child and physically insert her into the car and drive her home against her will. She was, however, tempted!

"Tell you what," Bruce suggested. "I've got to bring some papers out to Aunt Annetta. I was going to do it after church tomorrow, but what say I come tonight? You can send clothes back to town with me, and the girls can have a sleep-over."

Aunt Annetta is so right about Bruce.

Rebekka gave her a friend a silent question, only to receive a nodding response.

"Okay, little lady," she said to Aimee, after she'd gotten down on her child's level. If we let you stay and spend the night, there are three conditions."

"What are conditions, Mommie?"

"Conditions are things you have to do for us, if we let you stay."

She could see the wheels turning in her child's head, and finally she said, "So what are the conditions?"

Rebekka made certain her daughter was seeing her as she spoke. "First, you are on your best behavior and mind Miss Patti and Mr. Bruce. Second, no staying up all night playing. We all have church in the morning. And third," and here she hesitated, "when church is over tomorrow, you're going home to *High Lonesome* with me. No questions asked, no discussion, and for certain no temper tantrum like you almost threw here tonight."

Aimee was quiet for so long, her mother feared for what her answer would be. Finally, the little girl threw her arms around her mother, and Rebecca heard whispered in her ear, "I love you, Mommie."

At that moment, Rebekka's heart broke for the woman who had been so ugly to her on the phone only a few hours earlier. Anyone who saw Darryl even once would recognize that Aimee was his child. That his mother would question her parentage was beyond low and cruel. But it was what it was.

You're cheating no one but yourself, Judith. I pray that before you leave this world, you can recognize what a wonderful little girl your granddaughter is. She deserves to have a grandmother, although she's happy as things are. She can't miss what she doesn't know, and there are others here who are willingly taking your place in her life. I just hope you can realize this before it's too late.

Back at *High Lonesome*, she found Aunt Annetta in somewhat of a most unfamiliar sense of panic. The older woman was roaming the kitchen, opening cabinets and the huge zero-degree freezer and matching refrigerator.

"I totally forgot that I promised Emma the evening off. Her sister and her husband are celebrating a special wedding anniversary, and I wouldn't deny her the opportunity to go and be with her family for anything."

"So what's the problem?"

The woman regarded her as if she had lost her mind. "What will we eat tonight? You and Aimee and me? Do you know how long it's been since I cooked?" She grinned uncomfortably. "I'm afraid Emma has me spoiled."

"Well for starters," Rebekka said, as Bruce came through the back door. "Aimee is spending the night in town with Merry Beth. Bruce brought you some papers, and will take Aimee's clothes back."

Which reminded her; she needed to gather those clothes. "You and Bruce put your heads together while I run upstairs." Then she favored the woman who had come to be so important to her, with a broad smile. "When I come back, after Bruce leaves, you and I will go out on the town. My treat."

"Oh, my dear," Aunt Annetta said, her words clearly in the form of a protest. "I couldn't allow you to do that."

Remembering Bruce and Patti's words, Rebekka said, "You're allowing me to be blessed."

She took the stairs two at a time and soon had toiletries, pajamas and Aimee's special lamb blanket named "Laa" and clothes for church gathered. When she returned to the main floor, Bruce and Aunt Annetta were leaving the kitchen, headed for the den.

"Perfect timing," he said to Rebekka. He reached for the overnight bag she carried. He leaned to kiss Aunt Annetta's cheek. "See the two of you at church tomorrow."

"So where shall we go?" Rebekka asked, as they stood in the wide downstairs hall. "You know the area better than I do. You pick."

"We're not going anywhere until I have a chance to freshen up and change clothes. As for where we're going, you select. Whatever your budget can bear, that's where we'll go." She headed toward the stairs. "Just give me about ten minutes."

After she left, Rebekka decided she might ought to take a look at herself as well, and by the time she made it back to the main level, Aunt Annetta was waiting. Patiently waiting, she realized. *Man, I would have been dancing a jig. Where does this woman get it?*

She continued to press, and finally her guest offered up the name of a place totally foreign to Rebekka.

"Gopher Junction? That's a restaurant?"

"I've never been there," Aunt Annetta confessed. "But I've heard good things. When you're solo, it's no fun going out to eat at places with interesting names. It just makes you remember all over again how alone you are."

Rebekka's heart was breaking, although she understood that Aunt Annetta was not trying to throw a guilt trip. The woman wasn't that way. There was no debating it. She'd been paid the previous day, there was no funeral home bill and no car repair bill to pay. Right at that moment, it didn't matter what this meal cost. She was going to treat Aunt Annetta to this special night out.

There were a couple of times when they were bouncing along a single-lane wide country dirt road, attempting to dodge the potholes, when Rebekka wondered if her GPS had misled her. But she didn't confide her fears to Aunt Annetta. Finally, through the darkness, in the edge of the trees, was a ramshackle old house that looked as if it would tumble in on itself, if even one good wind came along. Around the building, parked all manner of haphazard ways, were enough cars to overflow a small used car lot.

"My daddy always said never stop at a restaurant where the parking lot was empty at eating time. He said that was the best barometer of how good the food was."

"If he was right," Aunt Annetta said, "we're in for some good eating tonight." She took Rebekka's arm, as they picked their way across the rough and uneven terrain to the front door. "And while we eat, my dear, you must tell me more about your parents. I'm anxious to know them also."

Inside the restaurant, at tables arranged wherever there was available floor space, they found themselves seated at a small table for two by one of the front windows. While it appeared that no money had been spent to enhance or update the décor, it was obvious from the demeanor of their fellow diners that a shabby appearance didn't translate into the food, which Rebekka and Aunt Annetta were soon to discover for themselves.

"This mountain trout absolutely melts in my mouth," Aunt Annetta said, as she forked another bite of the succulent fish. I don't know what they seasoned it with, but it's superb.

Rebekka, who wasn't a big fan of fish, had ordered a steak. The first one she'd had since before Darryl's death, and even then, it had been the rare, special occasion kind of food. As Darryl had been fond of saying, tube steak was more their speed, and indeed, he had enjoyed his hot dogs so many different ways. And even though she missed him so badly at that moment, this was indeed a special kind of occasion.

"Maybe it's been so long since I've had steak I've forgotten what it's like," she said. "But this is so tender and full of flavor."

"You've had a hard year, haven't you, my dear?"

Rebekka had to grapple for control of her emotions before she felt safe to answer. "I never would have dreamed it could be so difficult." She put down her fork. "Not just giving up Darryl, but all those other matters that came about as a result."

"It's never easy to give up those we love," her dinner companion said. "I think perhaps it's one of the most wrenching experiences of my life." She paused, dabbed at the corner of her eye with her napkin, and continued. "There toward the end, we knew we were losing Jan. With A.J., it was sudden. One minute he was there, the next he was gone, too." More eye dabbing. "I can't honestly say that one was any easier to deal with than the other. The bottom line was the same: they were gone."

Rebekka was at a loss for words. She knew if she spoke what was on her heart their wonderful meal would dissolve into a crying jag for both of them. It was time to change the subject.

"Look what they've done with those Christmas wreaths. Isn't that a novel idea?"

That novel idea was mismatched antique empty picture frames hung at strategic places around the old house. Inside each frame, hung a different style wreath decorated to reflect the holiday season. None were exactly alike or even the same size, but the coordinated effect could be called nothing short of spectacular, Rebekka thought.

"They had a professional decorator to put all that together," Aunt Annetta said, her voice ripe with conviction. "To make everything match when nothing matches takes the trained eye of an artist."

They had finished their entrees by this point, and were enjoying the restaurant's much touted bread pudding. "We've got to get started on decorating at *High Lonesome,*" Aunt Annetta said. When Jan and

A.J. were here, we always had the entire house in Christmas mode by the end of the day on Thanksgiving. I'd say we're running late."

"You haven't decorated in all the years since?" Rebekka asked, as she calculated the correct tip.

"Emma and I would put up a small tree in the den, and we always hung wreaths on the front and back doors, but that's been about it." She favored Rebekka with a smile that lit the older woman's face. "But this year, we're going all out. Starting Monday morning." There was the smile again and it warmed Rebekka's heart. "My dear, you have no idea what a special Christmas this is going to be."

There was that reference to this year's Christmas being more special. Only Rebekka didn't understand why.

In the car, on the way back to *High Lonesome,* Aunt Annetta said, "Oh, dear, you were going to tell me all about your parents tonight. I'm sorry we didn't get to talk about them. They must have been exceptional people to have raised such an amazing daughter."

Rebekka was both complimented and humbled by the endorsement of her parents. Christmas was always such a painful time to remember them, most especially their loss. Talking about them would be difficult, but she felt in some strange way that she owed an explanation this woman who had literally adopted her and Aimee.

"When we get back to your house, I'll tell you about two of the most amazing parents a girl could ever have had."

A short time later, with the fire crackling on the hearth and the comfort of the den as a backdrop, Rebekka introduced Aunt Annetta to Helen and George Cochran.

"Dad was a vice president for a construction company and Mom was a fifth grade teacher. I was an only child."

"Did your parents spoil you?" Aunt Annetta asked, as she worked with a piece of needlepoint in her lap.

Rebekka stopped to consider her answer. "Spoil me? No, I don't think they did. But they did make it possible for me to take dancing lessons and go to summer camp, and do a lot of those things that make a difference in a child's life." She hesitated. "Those things that I want so badly to give Aimee. Darryl and I had already talked and he'd promised me that she would have those opportunities." Her hands, which hadn't stopped moving the entire time she'd been talking became suddenly still. "Now I wonder some days if I'm even going to be able to provide a roof, food and clothes. She deserves so much more."

"God has a way of providing, my dear," came the quick reply from the other chair. He will see that Aimee gets what she needs."

Rebekka was quiet, trying to process what had just been said.

"So you had a happy childhood?" Aunt Annetta was steering the conversation back to safer ground. "Did you have other extended family members? Grandparents?"

"I had a wonderful childhood. Don't misunderstand. I had

chores to do, and I did them, or I paid the consequences. But I never doubted that Mom and Dad loved me. They were both only children, so there were no cousins or aunts and uncles. Dad's parents lived in Arkansas, so we only saw them about once a year. Mom's family was from south Georgia, so I knew those grandparents better."

"I know losing your parents had to have been rough."

Rebekka nodded her head, momentarily unable to speak.

"The only thing more difficult was losing Darryl, and if he hadn't been there to hold me up when the folks died, I don't know how I would have survived." She halted and swiped her eye with the back of her hand. "He absolutely was my rock."

Again, the emotions of those horrible days overwhelmed her, and Rebekka had to go quiet.

"So how did you lose your parents?"

Rebekka had asked herself that question so many times. Even with the police report to substantiate everything, it still seemed like something unreal.

"Dad died in a freak accident on a construction site and Mom died a few hours after the funeral of a broken heart."

"Oh, my dear, how tragic."

"It hurt. Believe me. But another part of me is so thankful they basically went together."

"I can see how you would feel that way. It must have really hurt to lose them both at once."

She stopped, replaying in her mind's eye many memories of happier times, of her parents together. "They didn't just love each other. Each one cherished the other. If one of them had been left to fend for themselves alone, I don't know that I could have stood the unhappiness."

"You were an only child. You didn't even have brothers or sisters to help you grieve."

"They wanted other children, but Mom said in later years that God had given them one miracle. She felt like asking for a second one was being greedy."

"Children are indeed miracles from God. That's how A.J. and I felt about Jan."

"There were times growing up when I wished I'd had built-in playmates. But I never felt neglected or deprived."

"It sounds like your parents were as blessed to have you, as you feel, even now, to have had them."

"I just wish they had been here to know Aimee. It hurts me most that she doesn't have any grandparents to love her in that special way."

"Sadly, we can't always make people love us."

Her words made Rebekka remember that she'd shared all the

issues with Judith with Patti, but she'd confided very little to her new aunt. And even at this point, knowing what she'd learned earlier in the afternoon, she was loathe to trash her mother-in-law to a woman who had never met her.

"Darryl's mother and I never got along. Somehow or another, she blamed me for Darryl's death, although I've never understood how. She's so bitter, she's elected to shut Aimee out of her life as well."

"That poor woman must really be hurting."

"She is that," Rebekka said. "The problem is, she doesn't want to get past the hurting. And she's taking it out on the only grandchild she'll ever have."

'We must pray for her," Aunt Annetta said. "If ever a person needed prayer, she does."

Rebekka agreed that prayer was called for. Unfortunately, after the manner in which she'd been treated that afternoon, it was going to take a while before she could lift Judith Austin's name in prayer and be sincere. Aimee and Darryl were father and daughter. For her mother-in-law to make accusations to the contrary, then demand a blood test, was more than insulting.

Almost as if they both knew that vein of conversation that coursed down through the family tree had been exhausted, talk turned to the Christmas party and the decorations and the food, and finally, to Rebekka's cottage.

"Mr. Thompson assures me, my dear, there should be no

problem having you in there by this time next week."

"It's okay, Aunt Annetta." And at the moment, Rebekka realized that it was indeed alright that finishing the work had been delayed. "It will be ready when it's ready. I'm just so thankful that Aimee and I will have a place to call home. You just don't know."

The remainder of the weekend came and went. It was obvious when church was over that Aimee still wasn't wild about separating from her friend, but when Rebekka had bestowed "that look" on her, there had been only token resistance.

Monday was back to business as usual, but with the added twist of having to get up earlier, get ready for work and pre-school in a new setting, then get out of the house and get there on time. If they were fortunate, Rebekka reminded herself, they would get to go through yet another adjustment in only a week, when they were finally in their house. However she clocked in at seven-twenty-eight. Mr. Hawkins might not be happy, but she wasn't late until she was late.

When they arrived back at *High Lonesome* that afternoon, she and Aimee had been amazed at the transformation from plain house to a combination of Winter Wonderland and Santa's Workshop. There was Christmas everywhere they looked, and the big house had undergone a personality transformation.

"Oh, Aunt Annetta," this is beyond beautiful. How did you ever get so much accomplished in such a short time?"

"Most of what you see here has been carefully packed away

in the barn. We didn't have to start from scratch."

I hope that Jan appreciated what a fortunate young lady she was to have had parents that cared this much. Then she realized, and the realization troubled her some, that she had been equally-blessed. Perhaps not on so large a scale, but blessed nonetheless.

"We hired help from town today, and what you see is what we got. Are you pleased?"

"This reminds me of that big mansion in North Carolina. Mom and Dad took me there once at Christmas and it was decorations everywhere you looked. This looks just like that, just on a smaller scale."

"Then I take your words as a compliment, because I, too, have visited that same house at Christmas. It is spectacular, isn't it?"

Aime was still marveling at all the Christmas decorations, and Rebekka was trying to rein in her daughter's over-the-top excitement, when Aunt Annetta said, "You'll find decorated trees in both your rooms, and I took the liberty of hanging a wreath at your cottage in your front kitchen window that faces the road."

Rebekka hadn't noticed it driving by, but she hadn't been looking. Suddenly it was of paramount importance that she see for herself the first Christmas decoration to go up at her new house. "Come on, Aimee," she said suddenly, and without even debating what she was about to say, "Let's go see our house."

Once outside in the brisk weather that fairly screamed Christmas, she took off running down the drive, the half mile or so to the cottage that was soon to be her home. Just as she'd been told, there, hanging on the large window at the end of the kitchen, was the prettiest huge, green wreath with a red bow. Lights were on inside, and the glow from the window gave the entire cottage a magical glow.

If there were snow on the ground, this would be a perfect Christmas card picture!

Unable to resist going inside, Rebekka submitted to her wishes and they picked their way carefully across the porch that was littered with building materials and tools. "We need to be very careful in here," she reminded her daughter. "We don't want to get in the way of these men who're putting our house back together, and we don't want to get hurt, either."

"I'll be careful, Mommie," Aimee said, seemingly as enchanted with the little house as her mother.

"Ms. Austin," Mr. Thompson's voice rang out. Rebekka had to look to find him half-hidden behind the carton the dishwasher had come in. "It's good to see you this afternoon. Come to check up on us?"

Lest the contractor think she was being pushy, she said, "We came down to see the Christmas wreath Aunt Annetta hung on the window. But the lights shining through the window seemed to be saying 'come in'." She glanced around at all the chaos and confusion in the two main rooms. "I hope we aren't in your way."

"You just make yourself at home. But be careful, there's a lot to trip over in here." He favored Aimee with a smile. "I'd hate to see this pretty little girl get hurt."

After visiting another couple of minutes, Rebekka asked where, exactly the new dishwasher would go, then she and Aimee picked their way through the house and back to the door they'd entered. "We'd better go and get out of the way," she told Aimee, and the two closed the door behind them.

"Oh, Aimee," she enthused. "Can you believe it? In a few days, this is going to be our home?"

"That's right," she said, "our house. So will daddy come back to live with us then?"

A huge lump formed suddenly in Rebekka's throat, and although she knew what her answer to the little girl had to be, she also knew what her heart wanted to say. She knelt to her daughter's level, and said, "I'm afraid not, darling. Daddy won't ever be coming back to live with us, but you can be sure that up in heaven, he's so glad we're getting this little house just for us."

"But if he loves us, why doesn't he want to live with us? Doesn't he like our little house?"

Her daughter's questions, honest and forthright though they were, caused much angst in her heart that was already overflowing with questions and conflict, and too many contradictions to process in one seating.

She hugged Aimee to her as she said, "Daddy will always love us, sweetie. But he's just not able to live with us anymore. Which is why we must always remember him and keep him in our hearts."

As Rebekka rose to her feet, Aimee looked up at her and said, "I wish I understood, Mommie." The grief and lack of understanding in her daughter's words spoke to Rebekka's still aching heart.

You're not the only one, Aimee..

They made their way back to the big house much more slowly than they had run down. It was almost, Rebekka thought, like they were both reluctant to leave that little house and all the potential happiness it held for them.

The next week flew by with amazing speed, when compared to the list of tasks and needs that Rebekka had going. When compared to the list of items still remaining to be finished at the cottage, she was certain someone was shoving additional days into the calendar. Mr. Thompson had estimated the house would be ready for her by Friday. While she'd found him to be a man of his word, Rebekka was still hesitant, lest she be disappointed again.

When she came into the house, Aunt Annetta and the contractor were waiting. From the expressions on their faces, she sensed that more bad news was coming. There had obviously been another delay. *What could it possibly be this time?* There would be no moving this weekend.

"Hello, dear, we were waiting on you."

"I'm sorry, Aunt Annetta. I had to make that phone call before four o'clock, so I'm running late." She glanced at the huge clock in the hall way. "Looks like I just did make it."

"That's fine, dear. But Mr. Thompson would like for us to go to the cottage with him. He has a question for you."

"A question. For me? Can't you just ask it here?"

"I could," the contractor replied, "but I think it would be better if you saw it for yourself."

"Is this something bad?"

"Now we'll just have to trust him, won't we, dear?"

The three scrambled into the contractor's crew cab pickup truck and were soon pulling into the drive at the cottage. Every time Rebekka glimpsed the Christmas wreath hanging in the window, she received another thrill, almost like the cottage was her Christmas present. Aimee had asked for a doll house; her mother felt like she'd gotten that gift instead.

The first thing she noticed was that all the assorted tools and stacks of material that had been cluttering the porch were gone. That was a good thing, she decided. So what was this problem that required her to come and see and make a decision? She asked as much.

"It's this way," Mr. Thompson said, leading them through the kitchen, into the living room, and on into the hall to the two identical bedrooms. He flung open first the door to one room, then to the other. "My guys are in the barn right now loading up the rugs and the beds for these two rooms. Which room is yours and which one is Aimee's? They should be here any minute and we need to know where to set stuff down."

208

Rebekka looked frantically between the two. From Aunt Annetta's face, aglow with excitement, to the contractor's face patient, but still questioning.

"You mean it's done? The cottage is finished? We can move in?"

"You can if you can show the men where to place things," Aunt Annetta said.

She had already done all of that in her mind many times over since the first time she'd seen the inside of the cottage, and Rebekka wasted little time answering questions. In slightly more than an hour, the rugs were down in both bedrooms and the beds were assembled and the bedding was waiting to be made up.

It was like a dream come true, and Rebekka couldn't hold back the tears of joy that streamed down her face. It truly was like God was putting the puzzle of her life back together, one piece at the time, when He felt like the time was right.

"Emma will be down in a few minutes to make your beds and put towels and supplies in your bathroom," Aunt Annetta said.

"But I've got all those items."

"Yes, you do," Aunt Annetta interrupted. "But they're packed up in boxes in the barn. This way, you and Aimee can sleep here tonight. Isn't that what you want?"

We can sleep here tonight! How dense can I be?

She threw her arms around the older woman and hoped the hug she delivered adequately conveyed how much this adoptive mother had come to mean to her.

They were going to be at home that very night. Now she had to arrange to get everything else brought down from the barn.

As if she were reading Rebekka's mind, Aunt Annetta said, "Tomorrow morning, members of your Sunday School class will be here to bring in everything else and help you get situated. Patti's got it all organized."

Patti!

"Patti knows about this?" she asked. "She's got it organized?"

"Don't be angry, dear. If we were going to surprise you, we had to tell someone. Who better than Patti?"

Who better indeed!

By the time the subject of their conversation arrived with Aimee, everything was shaping up for a first night in their new home. Rebekka had been so stunned by the events unfolding around her, until she'd actually forgotten to go back to town to get Aimee. It hadn't been until her daughter burst through the door, followed closely by Merry Beth and Patti, that she realized how derelict in her motherly duties she'd been.

"So they tell me you knew about this before me? That's grounds for… for… well, I'm sure it's grounds for something."

"It's grounds for saying 'Welcome home!' And before you get too bent out of shape, I didn't know it until about ten o'clock this morning when Aunt Annetta called me. So see, I haven't even seen you since you dropped Aimee off this morning."

"Sounds like to me you're splitting hairs, but I love you too much to be angry for long." She rewarded her friend with a huge hug. "Oh, Patti, can you believe it? We're finally here. I didn't think I could ever be this happy again after I lost Darryl."

As the two collaborated once again over where the remainder of her furniture would go, the housekeeper arrived to put the beds in order. Aimee and Merry Beth had been shooed out of Aimee's room, and they came back into the living room.

"Mommie? Can Merry Beth sleep over tonight?"

"Oh, darling," Patti said, "not tonight for your first night in your new house? You'll be out of school soon for the Christmas holidays, and you guys will have plenty of time to play with each other."

"But I want her to stay tonight. It's only special on the first night."

She's right, Rebekka thought. There are so many firsts in our lives. And she's experiencing one in her life she'll remember until she's an old woman.

"We don't have everything ready, Merry Beth, but if you don't mind sort of camping out, we'd love to have you help us christen our new house tonight."

She looked to Patti. "We might as well face it. These two have become as close as sisters, and for the next few years, they're always going to be together, at one house or another. Might as well start it off right tonight."

In the end, Bruce joined them with pj's and clothes for Merry Beth, and they all adjourned to the big house where Emma had a huge pot of chili, green salad, garlic toast and pecan pie waiting. It was a meal truly to remember, made more so by the spirit of celebration that fueled the festivities.

They bathed the girls and got them into their pajamas, then Rebekka showered and got her gown and robe and slippers. Everyone, except Aunt Annetta and Emma, had formed an impromptu two-car caravan down the drive to the little cottage Rebekka had nicknamed *High Anticipation*, and dropped them off for the evening.

"We'll see you guys in the morning by ten o'clock," Patti said, after she and Bruce had kissed their daughter and were preparing to leave. "Sleep well, because we've all got a hard day of work tomorrow." She glanced fondly around the inside of the cottage that had finished out much better than even Rebekka had dared to hope. It literally screamed cozy and sheltering and nurturing, and Patti was thrilled for her friend. "But when it's over, it's all going to be worth the work."

It certainly is going to be worth all the work to be able to call this little cottage my home. Somehow or another, she got the idea that Aunt Annetta had probably given her a life-time lease. That was comforting.

As she drifted off to sleep a little later in the evening, after making sure both girls were situated, Rebekka thought of the other firsts in her life, and like Aimee, would have to rank this night in the top five along with meeting and marrying Darryl, Aimee's birth, the first Christmas she could remember, and asking Jesus into her heart.

It wasn't until after her feet his the floor the next morning in the light of a new day, that she remembered one crucial matter. They had no food in the house, absolutely nothing for breakfast.

You should have realized this last night, dummy!

The girls would be awake at any moment, and would not be as flexible as adults could be in the same situation. She knew the problem; the issue was how easiest to resolve it. That's when a knock came from the kitchen door, where she found Aunt Annetta's housekeeper with a huge basket of food.

"Miss Annetta thought you and the girls might like to have breakfast together in your new house. Here's everything you should need, and if I've forgotten anything, just call me. I'll run it down."

She took the heavy basket from *High Lonesome's* housekeeper and set it on the counter nearby, before she rewarded the woman with a hug.

"You and Aunt Annetta always think ahead and have been so good to me. How can I ever repay either of you?"

"Miss Rebekka," the domestic said, "I've watched that sweet woman die a little bit every day since Jan and then Mr. A.J. died. It broke my heart, but there wasn't anything I could do. Since you came into her life, she's like a different person." She lifted the hem of her apron and wiped her eyes. "It's me who should be thanking you."

Neither of them spoke again for a couple of minutes, as each struggled to maintain her composure. Finally, Emma said, "So get those girls up and you all enjoy breakfast. Your workers are going to be here before you know it."

Oh, my gosh! How could I forget?

The Sunday School class was due in… she ran back to her bedroom to check her watch she'd left on the window sill, since she had no nightstand. Nine-oh-five. Less than an hour! She raced into the girls' room, got them up, and into the kitchen, where they sat cross-legged on the floor, Indian style, to enjoy the food.

When the first vehicle pulled up at almost ten o'clock, everyone was fed and ready.

The next few hours were a blur, as the ladies took over the house, cleaning, vacuuming, dusting, putting down shelf paper, giving the windows that looked out onto one of the most beautiful views Rebekka had ever seen one more wipe down, and beginning to unpack boxes and store the contents where Rebekka indicated.

The guys on the other hand, were back and forth from the barn bringing the remainder of the furniture, laying the rugs, placing the big pieces, and in short, helping wherever they were needed. Patti went to her car and brought back the framed Andrew Wyeth print and stood it on the mantle on the living room side of the massive stone fireplace. To the last person, everyone agreed that Mr.

Wyeth's depiction of a country keeping room was the element that tied everything together.

"It's perfect," Rebekka continued to exclaim, as first one element of the finished scene in the house presented itself to her. "I still can't believe all of this has come together."

Finally the emotions of the moment overwhelmed, and she began to cry. Tears of joy, sadness and grief, gratitude and love and even tears for the unknown still to come. Rebekka had to stifle herself before she dampened the enthusiasm of the group that had been so generous, and began to think she didn't appreciate all their hard work.

I told Aunt Annetta that I wanted a home for us and a family, as well as a secure future for Aimee and me. It looks like I've definitely gotten the first one. All these folks are our family because they've made themselves a part of us. If I don't get the third wish, I won't be disappointed. Who of us can foretell the future?

She looked at those around her and smiled. Who indeed could know what tomorrow might bring?

CHAPTER NINE

THE SPECIAL CHRISTMAS

Rebekka loved her job, but the prospect of leaving the stone and frame cottage each morning to venture in to town to work was heart-wrenching at best. She found herself straining forward in the driver's seat as she approached the *High Lonesome* gateposts each afternoon. Suddenly the phrase "coming home" held new and dearer meaning for her. She often had to pinch herself to be sure she wasn't in one gigantic dream.

The days slowly fell off the calendar. Finally, it was the last day of school until after New Years. As Rebekka straightened her classroom on that final day before Christmas break, and laid out work and supplies for when she walked back into the classroom next, she was mindful of all that had happened in her life in the year about to end. She prayed the New Year would bring additional joys and successes. She was privately proud of how well she had done, adjusting to single-motherhood and the crippling grief that had accompanied Darryl's death.

Oh, Darryl, please be happy for me that I've been able to move on to this point. I will always love you, and I will always miss you. I don't want it to seem that I no longer care for you.

In the early days of widowhood, she had often passed the darkest hours of the night talking with her husband. Sometimes expressing her love, often sharing a problem or a decision she had to deal with, and, on occasion, telling him how very angry she was with him for leaving her like he did. As she liked to point out to him, she and Aimee had been out grocery shopping when he left for work that last evening. She hadn't even gotten a chance to kiss him, tell him goodbye, or show him how much he meant to her.

It was a closure point she often wondered if she would ever achieve. He had meant the world, and she hadn't gotten to make sure he understood. And she never would, unless those middle of the night one-way conversations could deliver the message.

At home, she relaxed all the schedules and rules. There would be time enough for regimentation once school took in again come January. She and Aimee slept until they wanted to get up. They ate what they wanted, when they wanted. And if they wanted to curl up together on the couch and watch a movie until one o'clock in the morning, they did. Merry Beth was often in on the fun, and when she wasn't there, Aimee was at her friend's house.

One or two nights a week, Aunt Annetta had them to eat in

the evening, and often included Patti and Bruce and Merry Beth. Oh, yes, Rebekka told herself. She'd gotten her family that she'd asked for. It just didn't look like the family she had long envisioned.

Over the dinner table each time they gathered, Aunt Annetta positively bubbled as she recounted the plans and preparation for the Christmas party, and while Rebekka still didn't quite understand why this party and this Christmas was supposed to be extra special, she decided it must have something to do with what was in Aunt Annetta's heart. She decided to stop questioning and just accept that this would be a most special Christmas.

Finally it was just four days before the party. After consulting with Patti, Rebekka had taken Aimee to a professional photographer in Atlanta, and had a formal portrait of the two of them made as a gift for her new aunt.

"Face it, Rebekka," Patti had said, "there's nothing she doesn't have that she can't buy for herself. She will always treasure a picture of the two of you, especially if you should ever leave Cedar Mountain and move on elsewhere."

Leave Cedar Mountain? Move!

In all of her thinking and planning, Rebekka had never even considered the possibility that she might not grow old in this mountain community that had welcomed and embraced her when she needed those emotional hugs the most. But as she'd thought about it driving into the city, she grudgingly had to admit that Patti might have a point. What if the school didn't renew her contract? What if she got a much better job offer elsewhere? What if, and this was a long-shot, she fell in love again and re-married? It would be so good for Aimee to have a father. Not that any man could ever love her daughter more than Darryl had.

The prospect of leaving the mountain was totally foreign and distasteful, and while way back in her mind, she had to admit such was a remote possibility, she didn't want to entertain such negative thoughts at Christmas. So when the photographer said smile, Rebekka tried to make her facial expression match the joy she felt in her heart. Aimee, who never made a bad picture, was precious as always, and as she scanned the proofs, she knew Patti had spoken the truth. Aunt Annetta would treasure the picture. The future could do whatever the future wanted, and there was nothing she could do to change things. Hadn't she already learned that lesson more than once over the past year?

The first snowflakes began falling two days before the party, and before Rebekka could pull herself away from the many windows in her house that brought the outside in, the ground was already covered in white. Rebekka donned her coat and boots and ventured out onto the porch, then down the steps, to stand in the driveway and take in the tableau of her little house blanketed in a deep covering of snow. White and pristine snow that lent a magical quality to everything it touched.

As the day progressed, the accumulation became deeper, and the transformation of the landscape continued to evolve, until her cottage didn't even closely resemble what it looked like without the snow. Rebekka chastised herself for not taking a progressive series of photos, to document how the metamorphosis occurred. But there was no way to turn back the clock. Perhaps she would still be living here the next time it snowed like this, although the TV weather folks were calling this storm one for the record books.

Despite the snow, Aunt Annetta declared that the party would happen as planned, and even sent Bruce in the farm's four-wheeler to collect the two ladies from the cottage, along with their huge, gaily wrapped package that caused Rebekka to wonder if Aimee would be able to keep the secret until time to exchange gifts.

Inside the big house, Rebekka was surprised to see all the people who'd come in response to her aunt's invitation. Many of them she knew, most of them she recognized, however putting names with those faces was another matter entirely. But there was one gentleman who looked so very familiar to her, although she wasn't able to connect him with any business or any encounter she'd had in Cedar Mountain. This bugged her, as she knew it would, but soon the excitement of the evening built to such a crescendo, she momentarily forgot her perplexing mystery. His identity would come to her when she least expected. It might even be several days down the road.

The buffet was fantastic. Aunt Annetta had engaged a caterer to handle all the food, so that Emma, who was as much family as any person there, could enjoy the evening as well.

That's how gracious and concerned Aunt Annetta is. Lord, you know how good she's been to me.

Finally, it came time to exchange gifts, and to the surprise of no one, except the two youngest guests, a white-bearded old man dressed in red suddenly materialized in the doorway.

"Santa Claus!" Aimee and Merry Beth squealed in unison. "It's Santa, Mommie," Aimee exclaimed, as she and her friend rushed to embrace their visitor around the knees. The jolly old elf disentangled himself from their grasp, dropped into a nearby armchair, and invited both girls to join him. For several minutes, he talked with first one, then the other.

"These girls have decided they'd rather wait until Christmas Eve for me to drop off my gifts to them. But I understand that several of you have brought gifts tonight, so if I may invite myself to play master of ceremonies, I'm going to hand out the presents."

"Please do, Santa. We'll be forever grateful that you took time out of your busy schedule so close to Christmas," Aunt Annetta said.

"Ah," Santa commented, as he moved toward the tree anchored with gifts arranged around the base, "this promises to be a most special Christmas. I wouldn't miss it."

Santa engaged the girls to be his helpers, and in short order, all the gifts under the tree had been distributed. To the surprise of none, the biggest pile by far belonged to Aimee and Merry Beth. Rebekka knew Aimee had gotten Merry Beth a doll that was especially popular, and Aunt Annetta had given her a paint by numbers set. She was anxious to see the other gifts. Never had her child been so showered at Christmas. She wished Darryl were here to enjoy the scene that stretched before her eyes.

Before the girls could tear into their pile of treasure, Santa asked for everyone's attention. He called Rebekka's name specifically, and asked if she would accompany him to the nearby library, where her main Christmas surprise was being kept.

"Go ahead and let the girls open their presents," the old gent instructed. "And you folks feel free to open your gifts as well. Bruce, you take over for me."

"Will do, Santa." Bruce saluted smartly, before issuing the challenge. "Okay, girls… let's see who can open her presents the fastest. We'll have a prize for the winner."

As she accompanied Santa who suddenly, it appeared, had lost at least some of his joviality, she was surprised to realize that Aunt Annetta and the stranger from earlier in the evening, the man she still couldn't identify, were walking behind them. Aunt Annetta was holding tightly to the man's hand, and appeared to be stressed. Rebekka didn't know how to interpret her aunt's body language.

When they were all seated in the library, the other man got up to close the door, and in doing so, provided Rebekka with a profile that she immediately recognized. He was the man pictured on the security footage from the garage. She saw the distinctive scar. So was he also the man who had paid off Darryl's funeral? In her mind, he was. But why was he here tonight? And why were they all together in the library, away from their guests?

When everyone was ready, the stranger reached into his case and withdrew a folder of papers Rebekka estimated to be at least an inch thick. He laid the folder on the table, glanced at Aunt Annetta, who, Rebekka realized, nodded ever so slightly. Then he looked directly at Santa, and said, "Why don't you begin?"

Obviously, everyone here knows something I don't.

Santa tented his hands in front of him on the table, looked her way, and said, "Rebekka, we have some news to share with you tonight that we know will come as a shock. We hope, in the days and weeks to come, some of that shock can dissipate into pleasure and enjoyment. But before we tell you what we have, I'd like to ask you some questions. If I may?"

By this point numbness had begun to penetrate her, and Rebekka could do no more than nod her head in the affirmative.

"By the way," the red suited man said, "this other gentleman whom you don't know, is Harvey Walker, your aunt's lead attorney. He'll step in shortly."

For the next few minutes, Santa peppered her with questions about where she was born. Her earliest memories of growing up. Any other siblings. Anything her parents might have shared, either intentionally or unintentionally, about any unusual circumstances surrounding her birth.

Rebekka answered each inquiry as completely and as honestly as possible, wondering all the while where this conversation was leading. Was Aunt Annetta "disowning" her at Christmas? Had she done something wrong? Had her parents done a wrong against this woman who had been nothing but encouraging and supportive? There had to be a deep-seated reason for all these blunt and pointed questions.

Finally, when Santa indicated that he was satisfied, whatever

224

that meant, he glanced at the attorney, while she glanced at her aunt, pleading in her heart and mind and eyes that some kind of explanation be offered up. And soon!

"Rebekka," the lawyer said, fingering the file folder before him and flipping it open. "That's a beautiful name. Do you happen to know how you came by it?"

Rebekka had long admired the spelling of her name, but had never been able to get her parents to tell her where they got it? "I don't have a clue," she confessed. Then added, "But I've always wanted to know."

"Rebekka with this unique spelling was your great-grandmother's name. Your mother's grandmother, to be exact."

The minute she heard his words, she knew he was wrong. And probably whatever agenda this meeting had, they had the wrong person. "No, sir. My great-grandmother's name was Minnie Rose."

"That's your mother, Helen Burns Cochran's grandmother?"

"Yessir."

From the seat across from her, Rebekka saw Aunt Annetta begin to openly sob and tremble, and her own soul wondered what good could possibly come from is meeting. Part of her wanted to race around the table and fold the obviously distraught woman into her arms, and tell both the men to back off. It didn't matter if one of them was Santa Claus!

"This is going to come as a shock to you," the lawyer said, and there's no easy way to share this kind of information."

Rebekka steeled herself, and later, months later, there were moments when she still questioned if any of what had transpired in that room the night of that wonderful Christmas party had actually happened.

"Helen Cochran, the woman you regarded as your mother was, in reality, your adoptive mother. Your biological mother is sitting across the table from you, and is praying that with help from God Himself you won't reject her."

Rebekka had heard the expression "struck dumb," but she'd never appreciated the condition itself until she found herself trapped inside it. Her lips were moving, she knew that. But no words were coming out.

Finally Santa said, "Would you like to know more? Would you like to adjourn this meeting until another time? Tell us what we need to do to make you comfortable."

"But who? How?" She felt the room spinning about her. "I just don't understand any of this."

The lawyer pulled from his packet two identical sheets and handed one to Santa. "Your aunt was afraid when the time came, she would have difficulty explaining it adequately. She's written this letter to you, instead. Santa is going to read from his copy. He slid the other copy across to her. "Here's your copy so you can see that what you're hearing is what my client wrote."

Rebekka glanced at the letter, without really seeing anything on the page. Everything was a blur. Taking her lack of protest to be a yes, Santa began to read. The story that unfolded was one that Rebekka, whose dream was to write fiction, could never have created on her own.

Dear Rebekka, Santa read.

As I write this letter to you, please know that I understand how severely this news is going to impact you. I only hope that sharing the truth won't cause you to feel any less love toward George and Helen Cochran who reared you, and who, by the way, did a marvelous job. I can never repay what they've done. And I hope it won't cause you to cast me aside, at least not until you understand what happened and why I acted as I did.

I was a sixteen year-old unwed mother. Your biological father claimed to love me immensely, until he got what he wanted. After that, he didn't know I existed. I had fallen for his line, because there was so little love and no respect in my home growing up. When he told me he loved me, I was determined that he wouldn't get away, even if I had to give myself to him to keep him.

I was a conquest for him, the latest notch in his belt, I was soon to learn. Without him to provide for me, I had no choice but to confide the news to my parents, who promptly kicked me out. I sought refuge with my grandmother, who embraced me, loved me, never judged me, and was with me when you were born. Her only stipulation for her help was that I couldn't keep you, because in her ways that were so much wiser than mine, she realized neither of us had the financial means to provide for you.

There was just one stipulation that I placed on the adoption. I promised to never contact them or you, and in exchange, they would name you Rebekka, which was my grandmother's given name. I owed her that much. I met George and Helen once before you were born. They seemed like genuine, salt of the earth people, and as painful as it was to have you taken from me after I'd only held you once, and then for only a few seconds, I consoled myself that I had done my best by you.

By this point, Rebekka noticed, her own tears were flowing as profusely as Annetta Bigham's. No longer were the words on the page legible.

I went on to finish high school and college, but I never moved back to my parents. You don't know how many times, how many nights, I wondered and worried about you. Then I met A.J. Bigham, and we fell truly in love. You see, I understand how deeply you miss Darryl, because that's how I felt about A.J. He proposed, but before I would agree, I made him listen when I told him about you and all that happened. He insisted that it made no difference to him, so we were married. Occasionally, we'd talk about trying to find you, but I didn't want to be unfaithful to the agreement I'd made, so he held off.

Then I discovered I was pregnant with Jan, and I couldn't have been happier. Not that Jan could ever replace the baby I'd given up, but I felt like God wasn't angry with me, and that He was giving me a second chance.

As I think you know by now, Jan was one very loved little girl. Then when she was barely into her teens, we got the devastating news no parent ever wants to hear. Cancer. Leukemia. My very world crashed about me. We did everything humanly possible to save her, but shortly before she would have graduated from high school, we lost her. We actually willed her to die, and we both gave her our blessings to go on whenever she was ready. Giving you up and then giving her up were two of the hardest things I've ever done. Little did I know what was still ahead.

Rebekka couldn't bear to look at this woman who was proclaiming herself to be her mother. Not because she didn't believe, but because she did. The pain of losing two children was overwhelming.

A.J. was never the same after we buried Jan, and on the first anniversary of her death, he took his own life. Spelled it all out in a note, explaining that the loss hurt worse than any one human could hope to endure. There I was alone in the world. Two children gone, and now the man who had been the best thing in the world for me gone with them. Grief was a heavy load to bear. But somehow, with God's grace and my family, and members of our church, I managed to keep my head above water.

About two years ago, it occurred to me one day that I was absolutely alone in this world. The sad part about it to me was that I would have to leave my estate to faceless charities instead of giving it to someone I loved. I decided to try and find you. At that time, I had no intention of ever reaching out to contact you. I just wanted to know that you were okay, where you were, that I could see you from a distance, and when the time came, I could give you a nice surprise.

Only I wasn't counting on you being so lovely, such a fine young woman and wife and mother. Once we found you, I had to at least see you in person. I traveled to Atlanta and accomplished that dream. You never knew I was within fifty feet of you and Darryl and Aimee at the park one afternoon.

I managed to restrain myself from contacting you, though Lord knows my heart wanted to so badly. I had already learned that George and Helen were gone, so I felt like my commitment to them had become null and void. But on the advice of Mr. Walker, I did nothing. When I learned that Darryl had been killed, my dear, I knew exactly how you felt at that moment. I wanted to race to you, to hold you and comfort you, much as most mothers would have done. I know Helen would have, and I would gladly have stepped in to substitute for her.

In the weeks following Darryl's death, I kept closer tabs on you.

Gosh, Rebekka whispered to herself. Was she stalking me? The concept made cold chills march helter-skelter over her body.

Almost as if Annetta Bingham had anticipated such a reaction, her letter continued. *Please don't feel that I was stalking you, Rebekka. I only wanted you to be cared for. So when I learned that you were on financial hard times, and needed a job, I funded the local school system the money to hire you for two years, with the option to renew. I thought if I could just get you and Aimee to Cedar Mountain, then you would be taken care of, and I could see you casually around town. No one would ever need to be the wiser. I thought I could live with having you always at arm's length.*

But I didn't count of the force of a mother's heart. When Aimee enrolled in Patti's class, I felt like God had answered my prayers. Patti and I have always been very close; as you know she and Jen were like sisters, much as Aimee and Merry Beth are now. I encouraged Patti to bring you here to High Lonesome, *and once you were where I could touch you, hug you, and kiss you and do for you, I knew I had to reveal myself.*

I trust you won't think this old woman foolish, but I've come to love you for you. The fact that you're my daughter is just an added plus.

Santa stopped reading at that point. Do either of you ladies need anything before we finish this? He said to Rebekka, what remains in this letter all relates to legalities and estates. Quite frankly, I'd like to hear from you at this point, because I would feel I had done my good friend here a grave disservice, if I allowed what you're about to hear to sway your decision in any way."

How did she feel? Sucker punched? Angry? Confused? Concerned? In a total daze? All of the above? That last option left her feeling more in "no-man's land" than any of the other possibilities. In the end, she knew she had to speak. She understood that her world, her life would never be the same. Was she glad or sad that this new information had been dropped on her?

"For starters," she said, and looked directly at the woman that she now knew was her mother, "I'm in a complete state of shock. So I hope that nothing I'm about to say will either offend or come back to hurt me." She reached across the table and took the other woman's hand in hers, stunned to find it so cold and trembling.

"George and Helen Cochran never gave me any hint that I wasn't their biological child. Naturally, now that I'm older, I can see how they steered conversations around my birth or the births of any other children onto a safer subject. But I could never," she banged her fist on the table, "I could never do anything but thank them and feel grateful to them for everything they did for me." She looked straight at Annetta Bigham. "You gave birth to me, but they gave me life every day they were on this earth. I couldn't have asked for better parents. I will never do anything to diminish or tarnish the memory I have of them."

She hesitated, and realized that Annetta was sitting with her fist crammed to her mouth, almost as if it were all that was holding her upright. "Now Aunt Annetta. You'll have to excuse me if I can't call you mother right at this moment. If you had come totally out of the blue at me with this information, I probably would have blown you off and sought a restraining order to keep you away." She smiled to try and soften her words.

"Being able to get to know you over the past few weeks, allows me to see you in a different light. For one thing, I know you to be the generous, encouraging person that you are. I've seen it in action too many times. You're the one who paid off the mortuary and got my car fixed. Mr. Walker is the man who delivered the payments." She grinned. "Mr. Goddard at the garage has a security camera over his office area. He showed me the picture of the man. Only until tonight, I didn't know who he was."

The attorney and his client exchanged a glance that clearly said "Oops!"

"My dear," Aunt Annetta said through her tears, those funds were spent because you needed help. Whether you accept anything else from me, that's my Christmas gift to you. And Aimee."

"If you'll give me some time," Rebekka promised, "I'm going to try to work myself into this. But it's not going to happen overnight." She hesitated, then plunged ahead. "Is it alright if I continue to call you Aunt Annetta, at least for now?"

"You can call me anything you wish, as long as you don't cut yourself and that precious little girl out of my life. I cannot tell you what a difference having you here as made for me."

Rebekka recalled the housekeeper's words only a few days before, about the drastic difference she'd noticed in her employer since Rebekka and Aimee had come into the picture. Obviously there was some validity to it all.

"Let's go ahead and finish the letter," Santa suggested. "Instead of reading this part word for word, I'm going to hit the high spots. You've got the entire letter, you can read it for yourself if and when you wish."

He went on to explain that in return for Rebekka's acceptance of Annetta Bigham as her biological mother, Rebekka would stand to inherit her mother's entire estate, with the exception of special bequests to her housekeeper, the church, and a couple of other local charities. The cottage where she was now living would be deeded to her immediately, and the remainder of *High Lonesome* would fall to her upon Annetta Bigham's death. There were also bank accounts, investments, stocks and bonds, and some other real estate holdings, some of which would be transferred now.

In return, all Annetta Bingham asked was that both Rebekka and Aimee remain in her life, even if Rebekka were to remarry and leave Cedar Mountain, which she was free to do.

"I lost you once. I lost Jan. Now that I've found you, I can't bear to have to pretend that you don't exist. And I pray, Rebekka, that you can forgive me for breaking this news at such a festive time of the year. It has never been my desire to hurt you at all."

Rebekka glanced at the clock on the wall above the fireplace. They had only been in there about twenty minutes. Why did it feel so very much longer? Why did she feel as if she had aged one hundred years in only a few minutes time?

"We need to get back to the party, but I'd ask that none of this be shared tonight. I'm not ashamed, and in truth, I want to shout it from the rooftops. But not tonight."

"I think that's wise," Santa said.

"I want to be the one to tell Aimee," she continued, " because I'm not quite sure how to approach it with a four-year-old."

"You don't have to tell her at all, at least not for a while," Annetta volunteered.

Rebekka measured her words carefully. "I want her to know, but I need to know how I'm going to explain it." She smiled at the woman who had both aged before her eyes and gotten even younger than when the conversation began. "She deserves to know what a wonderful person her grandmother is."

"What else?" Santa asked.

Rebekka fixed her eyes on Annetta. "Patti. What about Patti? Does she know?"

The response floored her. "Patti knows nothing, and won't until you tell her. Bruce, however, handles all my business affairs. He's known about you from the very beginning. But you can trust his discretion."

Obviously I can! All this time I've been around him, and he never let on that he knew more about me than I knew about myself. For sure he never told Patti.

All eyes were on them when they returned to the den, where an ocean of discarded wrapping paper and bows and ribbons formed the foundation for two little girls who were celebrating Santa's largess with great glee.

When she spotted her mother, Aimee leapt to her feet, dashed across the room, and shouted. "Mommie. Aunt 'netta got me a doll house. I told you she would."

Rebekka let her eyes roam over the room but saw nothing that looked even large enough to be a small doll house. "Well where is your doll house? Show it to me." She took her daughter's hand, prepared to be led to see the magical gift.

"You know the house, Mommie. It's upstairs in the playroom." She dashed away and came back holding a by now crumpled piece of paper. "This is my deed, Mommie. It says I own the play house upstairs. Mommie. I love Aunt 'netta."

Yes, Aimee, I'd say we all do.

Knowing everyone was wondering why she'd been pulled off to the side, Rebekka tried to make a joke of saying Santa had asked her to turn informant on everyone in the room, before he finalized his list. A few people laughed, but most of them returned her limp attempts at humor with a blank stare. Seeing the huge package with the portrait of her and Aimee still sitting, wrapped, beside the tree, Rebekka hastened to it.

"Aimee," she called. "Can you come here and help me give Aunt Annetta her gift from us?"

Her daughter abandoned her play with Merry Beth amongst the sea of shredded wrappings. The gift, was, Rebekka realized, almost as tall as her daughter, but Aimee handled it all with deft and a fair amount of dexterity. Her mother had been so fearful she would drop the piece and break it.

Aimee approached their host, who'd taken her customary seat in the den and who, to those in the know, and a few who might only suspect, appeared to be going through the motions while inside everything was in turmoil. Rebekka worried that the strain of all of this might have been too much. After all, it had been a very heavy night.

"Here Aunt 'netta," Aimee said, as she thrust the large, thin package toward the woman she knew only as her aunt. "This is from Mommie and me. Do you need help opening it?"

"Aimee," Rebecca cautioned. "Aunt Annetta is a big girl. She can open her own present."

"You know, sweetheart. I think it would be wonderful if you would help me open this. I can't imagine what it could be. But I'm sure it will be wonderful."

Without waiting for further permission or instruction, Aimee began ripping at the paper Rebekka had worked so hard to fashion into a stylish looking package. "Mommie says it's…" Aimee began.

"Aimee. Remember what I told you?"

"Yes, Mommie." She turned to her aunt. "You'll have to find out for yourself. Mommie won't let me tell you that it's a picture of me and her."

With that slip of the tongue, Rebekka buried her head in her arms and counted to ten, while the remainder of the room broke up into hysterical laughter."

Aunt Annetta bent over the package and hugged Aimee to her. "That's the best secret about a present I've ever seen slip out. Thank you, Aimee, for the big clue."

The duo made quick work of removing the rest of the wrapping, and everyone was soon gazing at the sixteen by twenty color portrait of Rebekka and Aimee.

"Do you like it, Aunt 'netta? I wanted to get you a doll, but Mommie said no."

Annetta pulled the child to her, hugged her, and said, "Darling, you could give me an empty cardboard box and I would think it was the greatest gift in the world." Over the top of Aimee's head, Annetta's eyes and Rebekka's eyes met, and the secret love that flowed between them at that moment was one that few in the room even saw. But Patti did.

"Huh? An empty cardboard box?" Aimee twirled around to confront her mother. "Who would give a dumb gift like that?"

"Aunt Annetta just means that anything you gave her would be so special, she'd love it." She surveyed the remains of the wreckage in the room. "Don't you folks think we need to do a little housekeeping TLC here before we lose someone in the debris?"

With many willing hands, it didn't take long for the den to return to its normal livable space. While she was out at the recycling bin out back, Rebekka realized that Patti had joined her.

"Something's going on, and I want to know what it is." She stomped her boot in a show of frustration that Rebekka had never seen. Even Bruce, it appears, knows all about it. But he won't tell me anything." She ran her lower lip out in a pout. "He says to ask you." With her mouth still in anger mode, she planted her hands on either side of her hips, and stood as if daring anyone to interfere.

"He does?"

"Yeah. So I'm asking."

Rebekka wanted nothing more than to confide in her newest friend, but the lateness of the hour and the emotional stress she'd been under were taking a toll fast and thoroughly. "Okay, you're right. Something is going on, and you have to believe me, I knew nothing about any of it until a few minutes ago."

"So spill it already," Patti persisted. "You know you can trust me."

Rebekka knew that her new friend, now elevated to blood cousin, was entirely trustworthy. But it was too deep, too complex, and she was too exhausted to even begin the story that night. Forget finishing it.

"You're going to have to work with me on this," she emphasized. "I'm not trying to keep anything from you. But when I tell you it's too much to get into at almost ten o'clock, you're just going to have to take me at my word."

"So if not now, when?"

"Tomorrow. After church. I'll drop Aimee at your house and you and I will come to the cottage. I promise to share everything then, and answer any questions you have." She stopped to consider the promise she'd just made. "At least, I promise to try to answer all the questions you have."

"Well, I guess." Patti's face suddenly lit up, and Rebekka could tell it was killing her best friend to be in the dark. "Is it good news or bad news? You're not leaving Cedar Mountain, are you?"

Rebekka thought for a second. "I guess, depending on your point of view, it could be either good or bad." At the expression of revolt that flashed across Patti's face, she hastened to say, "In my opinion, it's good news. But I guess in the end, you'll have to make that call. And, 'NO,' I'm not leaving."

She hugged her arms to her. "Come on. Let's get back inside

before we catch our death of cold out here." She thought of a jab and delivered it. "So if you thought you'd hold me hostage out here until the cold made me spill the beans, you've thought wrong." She grabbed Patti's hand. "Come on. Inside, now."

It was another hour before the party wound down to the point that Rebekka felt she and Aimee could begin to take their leave. She approached Bruce, who'd been assisting Patti, and asked him about delivering them back to the cottage. "You need to tell Patti she needs to get Aunt Annetta up to bed. The poor woman looks like she's about to topple over."

"Way ahead of you," he said quietly, as Patti asked for the attention of those guests still hanging on.

"Hey, folks. Hasn't this been a fantastic Christmas party? It brought back so many good memories for me of when I was younger, and we did this every Christmas." She reached for her aunt and pulled her to her. "Aunt Annetta wants to thank each and every one of you for coming. And she doesn't want me to tell you that she's not as young as she was the last time she threw one of these shindigs, and that her coach is about to turn back into a pumpkin."

The room began to titter in response to the lighthearted eviction notice they were all getting. "You know the Good Witch here won't consent to go to bed as long as there's one guest left in the house. So be considerate of your elders, and we'll see you next Christmas. If not before."

It appeared that no one took offense, and in a matter of a very few minutes, the crowd had emptied out, and the sounds of cars picking their way through the snow to the public road over a mile away insulted the pristine night air.

"Your wife has quite the gift for sticking a knife in the ribs and having the victim smile the whole time."

"Yep, that's Patti, all right." He pointed the nose of the four-wheeler in the direction of the cottage. *MY cottage. It has my name on it!*

"I'm really proud of her, you know." He concentrated on navigating an especially deep snow drift, before he said, "So how are you? All this hasn't been too much, has it?"

Somehow Rebekka had known that question would come. She answered with a question of her own. "So how long have you known who I was, and who Aunt Annetta is?"

Rebekka watched the set of his jaw harden, soften and relax, and harden again, before he said. "Harold Walker called me two days after Aunt Annetta first gave him his assignment."

"So you knew the first time we met in your car that Sunday morning a few weeks back things about me that I didn't even know?"

"Are you angry?"

"Not angry, exactly. More like super impressed. How you could be around me and Patti, and not even allow some small tidbit to slip by accident is impressive."

"It's what's required in my line of work. But if it makes you feel any better, this has been the most difficult piece of confidential client information I've ever had to sit on." He wiped his brow with an exaggerated motion. "I'm so glad that's out, even though Patti is probably going to make me sleep on the sofa tonight."

Rebekka couldn't hold back the laugh that gained life. "Tell her I said she'll know everything tomorrow that I know, and that she shouldn't punish you tonight."

"We'll see how that flies," Bruce replied, as he leaned to pull into the short drive to the cottage. She hadn't realized she'd left so many lights on earlier in the evening, but as they rounded the curve and the cottage, now her cottage, came into view, there was an absolute magical glow radiating out of the windows and around the little house. Almost, she thought, like a halo.

"Here we are," Bruce said, as he pulled to a stop, got off, and came around to help Rebekka down. Once she was on the ground, he lifted the now almost comatose Aimee from her seat, and placed her in her mother's arms. This one has had a big night. Like her mother." He grinned. "Rest well, tonight, he said. "Tomorrow is the first day of the rest of your new life."

It appeared to be getting colder, and Rebekka didn't engage in conversation, but got them both inside the house, to the warmth that was so welcoming. Aimee barely stirred, as her mother got her dressed for sleep and tucked into her bed. She planted a kiss on her daughter's head and quietly left the room.

The great room was still lit by the heavily-decked Christmas tree in the corner. It was the largest tree she'd ever had, and it was the first time ever to have a freshly cut tree. *It looks like this Christmas IS destined to be a Christmas of new firsts.*

Her shoulders ached, her entire body felt as if she were dragging heavy weights along behind. She craved the warmth and comfort and safety of her bed, but her mind wouldn't shut off, and she found herself unable to reconcile all that had gone down that evening by just going to bed and shutting her eyes and going to sleep. Instead, she plopped down on the couch, the very first piece of furniture she and Darryl had bought new, and proceeded to replay the conversation in the library.

There was only one thing she could say with any degree of certainty. She understood and believed all that had been shared with her earlier. But she was so far from having her mind and her heart wrapped around it all, she couldn't predict how long it would take for everything to sink in, and for her to own the resulting reality.

Honestly. This whole thing reads like a most creative work of fiction. I only wish I could have written something so powerfully compelling.

Finally, because she knew the next day was Sunday, and daylight would arrive whether she was rested or not, Rebekka took herself off to bed. Sleep wasn't as long coming as she had feared it might be, and as she closed her eyes and began her descent into oblivion, the one thing she kept seeing in her mind's eye while Santa was reading the letter, was the combined expression of fear and desperation on Aunt Annetta's face.

She truly feared I would reject her, but still, she was willing to risk that to be sure I knew the truth.

It was the truth, Rebekka didn't doubt it for one minute. Aside from the documentation, including her original birth certificate, there was the credibility of her birth mother. The woman had nothing to gain and everything to lose, had she decided to reject Aunt Annetta's confession. Whereas she could have left everything as it was, they all would have been quasi-family, and no one would have needed to be the wiser.

A mother, she decided, would stop at nothing to protect her child, to do what was best for her child. Annetta had done that once, when she handed the infant Rebekka to George and Helen Cochran. She had done it a second time that night.

Rebekka awakened the next morning to find that the world outside was strangely quiet. She couldn't see the clock and the light in the room looked funny. Was it possible she'd overslept? She sprang from her bed to get a better look around. Turned out it was actually ten minutes before time to get up, and when she looked onto the winter wonderland outside her window, she realized that new snow had fallen during the night. A considerable amount, if appearances were any indicator.

The weather people are already calling this winter front that stalled out over us the most snow in seventy-five years.

Questioning whether she could get her car out from under its blanket of ice and white, she went ahead to wake Aimee and get them both into the kitchen for breakfast. They might make church and they might not. Best to assume that all would be a go.

As they were enjoying their Sunday morning staple of fresh, hot, yeasty cinnamon rolls, Rebekka's cell phone rang. Caller ID showed Bruce's number.

"Hello, Bruce."

"Don't try to drive into town to church in your car. We got an additional eight inches overnight. I'll be out shortly to pick up everyone at *High Lonesome* in my four-wheel-drive SUV. See you in a few."

She heard Bruce going by to get Aunt Annetta, which made her wonder if she might feel strange or even uncomfortable being in such close proximity, before they each had a chance to come to terms with everything. For sure, both their lives had been turned upside down last night, and things would never be exactly as they had been before. As her mother had been fond of saying, once the toothpaste is out of the tube, you can't put it back.

When Bruce pulled into her drive, she and Aimee picked their way carefully across the snowy yard, to the back doors of the big vehicle. She was relieved, she realized, to see that Patti and Merry Beth were already there, and she breathed a silent sigh of thanksgiving. This would make things less awkward.

When church was over, Patti had informed everyone that they were all going back to her house for homemade vegetable soup and hot buttery cornbread. Despite protests to the contrary, Bruce soon pulled into his own driveway, and they all piled into the warm house.

Rebekka suspected collusion on the part of her best friend,

and confirmation came when the two of them were in the kitchen pulling together the food. "In this weather, I knew if you went back to the country, I'd never find out what's going on."

"I sorta thought you'd engineered this whole thing."

"Well, not the snow, I didn't." She held aloft the knife she was using to cut the cornbread squares, almost like a weapon. "I'm a mighty warrior with mighty powers, but even I can't make snow."

"But you can make it happen that we all end up in the same place to eat, so that you can get information."

Patti blew on the end of her sword. "You better believe it."

The simple country meal was filling and satisfying in more ways than one. It was after they'd finished off the homemade apple turnovers that had been their dessert, that Bruce set the course for the afternoon.

"Aunt Annetta, there are some loose ends you and I need to tie up from last night. Why don't we go into my study and we can handle all that here, before I take everyone back to *High Lonesome*?" He turned to the girls, "And why don't you two go downstairs to the playroom and enjoy yourselves. They're calling for more snow tonight, so it may be several days before you all see each other again." He said nothing to either Patti or Rebekka, although he did raise his eyebrows in Patti's direction.

The girls hadn't even waited for him to finish, before they hit the stairs headed to their own little world. Bruce had helped Aunt

Annetta to her feet, and they had disappeared down the hall, in the direction of the study Rebekka knew was in the back of the house.

She wondered how to bring the conversation about. Not that she minded sharing, but the question was where to begin. Patti, on the other hand, evidently had no such difficulty. "Come on," she said, and grabbed Rebekka's hand, "we'll have privacy in my bedroom." And without asking, she grabbed her friend's hand and began to drag her toward the stairs.

When she had an opportunity later to reflect on the conversation between herself and Patti that afternoon, she could but marvel at how natural it had felt to share such an unbelievable story. That bloodletting had also been the demarcation of the remainder of their relationship. No longer best friends, they were now cousins, joined genetically by their aunt. If anything, Rebekka decided later, their bond had been strengthened.

As Patti began to hammer her with questions as soon as the bedroom door had been closed and locked, Rebekka had simply held up her hand, and said, "Stop. I will tell you everything, but you must let me do it in my own way."

"Then spill it."

Rebekka took a deep breath. "I'm going to cut to the bottom line first. Then I'll go back and fill in the blanks." She noted Patti's restlessness, and knew she'd better move on. "Last night, I learned that not only were George and Helen Cochran my adoptive parents, something I never knew, but Aunt Annetta is my birth mother."

She would have paid good money for a picture of Patti's face when the news she'd just revealed hit her friend completely. In fact, she'd rarely seen Patti speechless, but that moment had been one for the record books.

Finally Patti attempted to find her tongue. "Now wait. Let me get this straight. Aunt Annetta, MY aunt who's downstairs with Bruce right now, is really your birth mother and not Helen Cochran who raised you?"

"Right."

"You wanna explain that?"

"Now do you see why I didn't want to get into this last night?"

"Okay. Yeah. I guess. Only get into it now."

"Rebekka shared all of the contents of the letter that she could remember. "I'll let you read my copy but I don't have it with me today."

"So you're telling me that Aunt Annetta gave birth to a baby before Jan was born and before she ever knew Uncle A.J.?"

"That about sums it up," although it doesn't begin to answer all the questions."

Rebekka suddenly had the uneasy suspicion that Patti might not welcome the new information, or the relationship that was bound to develop between Annetta and herself. "You're not angry at Aunt Annetta, are you? Or maybe jealous?"

The look Patti gave her made her fear her friend thought she had multiple heads. "Good grief, no. I'm just trying to get things fixed in my mind. So did Uncle A.J. know?"

"He did. She refused to accept his proposal until she'd confessed all, and gave him the chance to rescind his proposal."

"Obviously he must have accepted her explanation, because they did marry, and from everything I saw, were thoroughly smitten with each other up until the day he took his own life."

"He not only accepted her with what she considered a blemished past, told her it didn't matter to him. He even offered to find me for her."

"That would have been Uncle A.J."

Rebekka reflected on the man who had suddenly become the step-father she knew only by name and reputation. "I'm sorry I didn't get to meet him."

"You would have loved him and he would definitely have loved you. So what's next, Cuz?"

"Do you realize I've never had anyone to call 'Cousin' before?"

"Well you have now."

"So are you still mad at Bruce?"

"Of course not. I wasn't mad last night, either. Just wanted to make him think he was in trouble."

"That's a dirty trick. He was only doing his job, you know."

"Yeah, I get that. And there were changes that had to be made in all her accounts. He would have been the one to do that, so she had to confide in him."

"He told me last night he's known since the first day I arrived here in Cedar Mountain, who I was and all the details."

Patti got up from the foot of the bed where they'd been sitting and moved across to the big Palladian window that looked out over the back yard. "My gosh, it's snowing again. Can you believe it?" She let the drapery fall back into place and said, "If he's been able to keep all of this from me, I wonder what else he's hiding. I may have to interrogate him a little more closely."

"Now Patti, don't go…" Rebekka's words were interrupted by a shout from below.

"Patti, are you both upstairs? It's snowing again and I need to get the ladies back to *High Lonesome* before it gets any worse."

Rebekka jumped from where she sat and answered, "We'll be right down, Bruce." She headed for the door.

"Wait," Patti said. "What about you and Aunt Annetta? Are you going to be okay with all this? Is there anything I can do?"

Knowing they had to hurry, Rebekka rolled her words around on her tongue before she spoke them. "It still feels a little awkward. You know, weird awkward. I'm having trouble making myself even think of her as my mother. Forget calling her that."

THREE GIFTS FOR CHRISTMAS

"I'm sure she understands that. After all, it hasn't even been twenty-four hours since all of this fell on you. Don't beat yourself up."

"The very last thing I want to do is to hurt her in any way. She's been so very good to me."

"Come on, ladies!" they heard from the lower floor. "Father Time and Mother Nature wait for no one, least of all us."

The two ladies, cousins now, hurried to the main level. While Bruce and Aunt Annetta helped get Aimee into her coat and boots, Patti insisted on sharing the soup that had been left from lunch, and in a matter of minutes, the guests from the country headed out in driving snow with their plastic containers of vegetables and broth as well as left-over cornbread.

"Can you get us home and safely get back to town," Aunt Annetta asked Bruce, who was struggling to see through his windshield that was being pelted with what appeared to be baseball size blobs of white.

"Shouldn't be a problem," he assured them. However, from where they were riding in the back seat, Rebekka could sense Annetta's discomfort in the front passenger seat. Somehow she needed to diffuse that stress.

"I shared our conversation of last night with Patti."

Her mother's head snapped upright, and she turned to look straight at Rebekka. But nothing was said.

"She's thrilled," Rebekka said. "Said she'd talk to you about it later, but that she couldn't be happier."

As if Annetta had been given a massive muscle relaxant, in one motion, her entire body appeared to almost go limp. Rebekka feared for a moment that she might be about to faint.

Almost as if the troubles of the entire world had been lifted from her shoulders, and she'd been given an energy drink as well. Rebekka literally watched a new Annetta Bigham being created right in front of her eyes.

This has eaten at her all these years. Never mind that her husband forgave her, she's never forgiven herself until just now. Rebekka couldn't begin to imagine the inner torment this sweet woman had lived in day after day for more than a quarter of a century. *That's a long time to carry a burden. Especially a needless burden.*

"Aunt 'netta," Aimee piped up, "what are you all talking about?"

Rebekka had been so wrapped up in her mother's struggles, she'd actually forgotten that her little daughter with the big ears was right there in the car. She had originally intended to send Annetta a coded message that all was well. Nothing more. It was obvious that the older woman was struggling for an appropriate answer. If there was one.

"Well, you see, sweetie…"

"Aunt Annetta and I were talking about some people we know who have already been given the most precious Christmas gift and how happy we are for all of them."

"Oh." It was obvious that neither of them had answered Aimee's question exactly. In time to come, that would have to happen. But for the moment, just days before the official day of giving, a family had been united and formed, and it was indeed a joyous event.

"Here we are," Bruce announced as he pulled into the drive at the cottage and stopped the SUV. He came around to hold Rebekka's soup while she stepped out, then reached in for Aimee, whom he hugged as he sat her down on the ground. "You all hurry on in the house. As hard as it's snowing, you'll both be turned into human snowmen if you stay out here very long."

Aimee giggled. "Human snowmen, Mommie. Let's do it."

Rebekka accepted the plastic container of supper as she shooed her daughter up the path. "No ma'am, we do not want to become frozen snowmen people. Now walk carefully, but let's get inside where it's warm."

As she stood on the porch watching Bruce back out of the drive, she was struck yet again with the irony of all that had gone down. She had confided in the woman she knew at the time as the aunt of a friend, that all she wanted for Christmas was a home that belonged to them, a real family again, and the assurance that she could care for herself and Aimee in the years ahead.

At the time, her wishes had sounded rather flip, even to her. Yet that had been her wish list, based on the needs that she saw then. Suddenly, those three dreams had not only been answered, but it ways so much more magnificent than she could have ever imagined.

These were three Christmas gifts she would never, ever forget. If she had her way, no one else would, either.

EPILOGUE
SIMPLE GIFTS

B y the first week in January, all the legal paperwork that made Rebekka the legal heir of Annetta Bigham had been signed, witnessed, notarized, and filed away for future use. A future that Rebekka fiercely hoped wouldn't happen for many, many years. She'd already lost too many people in her life in too short a span of time. And she'd been deprived of her birth mother for so many years. She prayed God would allow them generous time together, to truly bond and enjoy their relationship.

Every day in the little cottage was a new experience. Whereas in the past Rebekka had been forced to propel herself out of bed every morning, the sunlight coming through the east window of her bedroom seemed to have a magical quality about it. Almost like the children following the Pied Piper, she was drawn from her bed to see and soak in and enjoy the essence of each new day. She couldn't wait to get started.

Aimee had settled in well to life in the little house in the edge of the woods, and several times a week, either Rebekka would take her to the big house, or Emma would come down to get her. The little child and the older woman would enjoy the play room and the playhouse for hours on end.

After several discussions with Annetta, it had been agreed that Aimee was too young to fully grasp the fact that Annetta was her grandmother, when in truth, she already regarded her as such. She would be given all the facts later, when she was old enough to understand. As for the new mother-daughter duo, their relationship was still feeling its way day by day. Not that there were problems, it was more like a merging of perceptions.

"It really bothers me," Rebekka had confessed to Annetta one day, as they watched Aimee preparing a meal for them in the kitchen of the playhouse, "that I can't call you mother or mom." She felt totally helpless and hoped her body language proclaimed her true feelings. "It's not that I don't want to, but when I go to say it, the words won't come out."

Annetta had patted her hand the most tenderly she ever remembered being touched. "It's alright my dear. The fact that you want to is enough for me. Remember, I told you the night of the Christmas party, I don't care what you call me, as long as you don't shut me out of your life."

Rebekka did remember. "But it still bothers me," she insisted.

A few days later, as she was shuffling through some papers on her desk, where she had begun to enjoy sitting to grade papers and do more exciting things, it came to her. The name was so perfect, she actually practiced saying it aloud several times. She loved the sound that hung in the air after she spun it off her tongue, and she felt totally free and at peace saying it.

This was something that couldn't wait.

She grabbed Aimee, who had been playing in her room, and

they headed to the big house. Aimee was shooed up to the playroom, which took absolutely no effort. Then Rebekka went in search of the lady of the manor, whom she found at her desk in the library.

"Rebekka, dear. It's so good to see you. You look like you're about to explode with excitement." She got up from her chair, came around the front of the desk, took her daughter's hand, and led her to the nearby loveseat. "Here sit and tell me what's up."

"I've got it," Rebekka babbled. "It came to me just a few minutes ago, and I had to share it with you."

"Now you do have my curiosity engaged. Tell me, quickly."

"Your name. What to call you." She was still babbling, stumbling over her words.

"You know I haven't wanted you to worry about that." She patted her daughter's hand again.

"I know," Rebekka said. "But when it came to me, it was just so perfect."

"Then, please, keep me in suspense no longer."

"Mom-Netta." She smiled with glee. "Isn't it perfect? Mom-Netta." She wanted to keep saying it over and over, until she could no longer make a sound. "I don't know where it came from, but don't you love it?"

Had she been more focused on her mother, and less on herself, Rebekka might have seen the color drain out of the other woman's face. The first clue she had that something was wrong was when her mother's arms wrapped themselves around her, and she realized that Annetta was sobbing. Not just sniffling, but actually crying as if her heart were broken.

As she attempted to comfort the woman, then to find out what she'd done to elicit such a response, she was startled to be asked, "Have you talked about this with Patti?"

Patti? What does she have to do with this?

"No ma'am, you're the first person I've said this to, and obviously I've done something terribly wrong. I am so sorry." She hugged her mother. "Please forgive me. We'll just forget all about this."

Annetta pushed away from her, tears still puddling in her eyes, but they weren't tears of pain or anger, Rebekka decided, if the smile on her face was any indication. So what was the problem?

"You had no way of knowing, my dear, and Patti may not even remember, but when Jan wasn't much older than Aimee is now, one of her favorite books was the story of a little girl who called her parents by their first names. It really made an impression on her, and suddenly we were Annetta and A.J."

She smiled through her tears, obviously remembering that time with fondness. "A.J. thought it was a hoot. Her name was actually Janie Annetta, so in return, her daddy called her J.A. One of the last words we heard from that precious child, just minutes before she slipped away from us, was "I love you A.J. Don't worry about me.

I'll be okay."

The memories were overwhelming, and Annetta had to stop and collect herself. "I realize now that I shouldn't have made such an issue out of what I was called, but I just knew what would have happened at my house, if I had called either of my parents by their given name." She shuddered, and Rebekka trembled herself, even though she could only assume how rough life at home must have been for her mother.

"Anyway," Annetta said, finally able to continue, "we struck a compromise. Jan came up with it herself. And while I didn't want to appear too enthusiastic, I actually liked it as well."

Rebekka felt herself go rigid. She knew without any doubt what was coming next.

"Mom-Netta. That was the name Jan chose for you."

As she felt her mother gather her into her arms, Rebekka could feel the woman's body giving way to a deep and cleansing cry that only happens a few times in a lifetime.

"The last time I was called that, before a few minutes ago, was when I was sitting, cradling her in my arms. She looked up at me and whispered, 'Bye Mom-Netta. I mean, Mother.' Then she was gone."

"Oh, Aunt Annetta," was all Rebekka could whisper.

"So you see, that's why I told you that night, I don't care what you call me. Just call me into your life and to be a part of your family. Right at that moment, when Jan left us, it wouldn't have mattered what she called me, just so long as I still had my little girl."

From that point on, Mom-Netta it had become. Rebekka had called Helen Cochran "mother," so it felt very natural and non-threatening to refer to her other mother as Mom-Netta.

As the school year progressed, her lessening stress load allowed her to become more in love with her students and the courses she taught. It finally came to light that the principal and Mon-Netta had dated a few times many years before. She had broken up with him to date A.J., and because she was funding Rebekka's position, the administrator had a private agenda.

It was, officials said, the worst winter on record in Cedar Mountain and the surrounding area. Rebekka could well believe it. She could count the total number of snows she'd ever seen before coming to the mountains on one hand. It took both hands and more than a foot to count the storms they endured that first winter in Cedar Mountain.

But as it always does, spring finally came. Whether the landscape was as tired of the cold and white as she was, Rebekka didn't know. But from every window in the cottage that had come to represent security and love, the view of blooming plants and trees was both colorful and profuse. The effect on her was almost as if an IV of spring fever had been pumped into her veins. She wanted to run and jump and yell and sing and, in fact, did a little of all. When she was alone of course.

The anniversary of Darryl's death had come, and she had taken off work and driven to Atlanta to the cemetery where his mother had demanded he be buried. Sitting on the ground beside his monument, she had shared with the man, who was still the love of her life, all that had transpired since that horrific night when he never came home.

She had left flowers, yellow roses because they were his favorite, in the vase attached to the stone. As she was getting into her car to leave, she spotted Judith approaching the grave, also carrying a bouquet of yellow roses. There was plenty of room in the vase for both her flowers and Judith's. As she watched, Judith jerked out Rebekka's roses, carried them into the edge of the woods and tossed them. Her body language had screamed venom and hatred.

Initially, Rebekka's response was that those were flowers that she had bought herself. She wanted to go back and confront the woman who had made it abundantly clear by her most recent actions that nothing Rebekka could do would bring about a change to Judith's hard heart. The woman was hurting, she knew. By her own choice, the only family she had was in that grave. A couple of hours up the road, Rebekka had more family that she could count. Since Christmas, as she'd gotten out more and engaged, she'd been amazed at the people who now called her friend.

She and Patti and Bruce had become very close. The label cousin simply made a great thing better, and she gave thanks daily for these people who loved and cared for her. And she was finding that as time went by, she and Mom-Netta were bonding more and more. It wasn't something they talked about. But it happened, and she was glad for it.

She felt sorry for Judith. All that she had in Cedar Mountain was something her mother-in-law would never experience, and the loss was all hers.

When school was out, after much prayer and talking with Mom-Netta, she had decided to revert to the plan she and Darryl had set into place when Aimee was born. Rebekka became a stay-at-home mom again. Income from some of Mom-Netta's investments she'd already put into Rebekka's name would yield enough, if she were frugal, and Bruce promised that he would see that she was, to pay their expenses for the immediate future. Maybe when Aimee was old enough to be in public school until mid-afternoon each day, she might go back to teaching.

In the meantime, Aimee continued to go to pre-school each morning, because she needed the socialization skills and would have felt she was being punished to be deprived of all her friends. But she came home at lunch, instead of going to extended care. Together, one mother and daughter and the other mother and daughter built a new life around and out of the ashes of past mistakes and grief.

As she sat at her desk in the alcove off the living room on that first fall morning when Aimee had gone back to pre-school, Rebekka stared at the open, blank text page on her monitor, and her fingers caressed the keyboard, hesitantly, almost as if she were fearful of committing to a stroke so strong it would actually cause the letter to appear on the screen.

It had been like this for weeks. She wanted to do this so badly, her body literally ached with need. But try as she might, she literally could not get her brain and her heart and her fingers all in sync. Nothing was working. She had bribed herself. Lectured herself, and even tried punishing herself, but her love of chocolate soon made denying herself the confection sheer torture. For certain the punishment didn't begin to fit the crime. In the end, she'd gotten down the calendar and circled the date when Aimee would go back to school. Until then, she had given herself a reprieve.

She and Aimee would enjoy the remainder of their summer vacation. There would be time enough for her new career once school was back in session. As she stared again at the screen, as her mind ran rampant over the lifetime of memories that had been crowded into the past year, she felt the spark leave her fingertips. With sure strokes and no hesitation, she watched, fascinated, as her hands raced across the keyboard and words filled the screen...

"Sometimes three gifts are all you need for Christmas, especially when they are the right gifts. After all, three gifts were all the Maji brought to Jesus...."

Coming in 2018 - 2019

In Service

Amanda Baldwin is an upstairs maid in the New York household of one of America's wealthiest families in 1905. While she isn't owned by her employers, she is nevertheless subject to their whims and dictates. When Amanda finds Jesus and invites him into her heart, she's shocked to discover that Christ isn't a welcome addition to the household. How she serves both Him and her employers is a story of conflict and contradiction, resolve and compromise. More than once, Amanda finds herself in the middle, asking, "What would Jesus have me do?" It's a journey Amanda undertakes with both fear and faith.

For Sale... or Not?

Business is good at Mountain Magic Realty by Mags. Following a brutal winter, when spring winds began to blow, showings and sales mushroom. More than once Mags finds herself unable to meet the demand, and toys with the prospect of bringing on another agent. When a distant relative of ex-husband Franklin applies for a job, Mags hires him despite warnings from her gut to step cautiously. Her new hire proves his worth and Mags relaxes. But is she becoming too comfortable too soon? Expensive mistakes on listings and contracts strain the relationship. Complaints from sellers and buyers about missing valuables and divulged private information create a whirlwind of conflict, accusations, broken relationships, and even threatened lawsuits. The private investigative firm of Gordon & Pickett must once again utilize all its gumshoe expertise to discover the who, what, why, and how of the potential destruction of Mags' real estate business.

Unwillingly Amish

When you marry someone, you marry their entire family. Constance "Connie" Miller knew this when she married the man of her dreams, who led her to believe that he had no family. After the "I do's," she discovers that he does indeed have family, and that he's also fully Amish, rebelling against his family and religion. When he ultimately demands that she live with him in his home community, conduct herself as a traditional Amish wife, and live a conventional Amish lifestyle, Connie feels her entire existence disappearing. Never mind that living the "Plain" life is totally foreign to everything Connie has ever known And the Amish religion flies in the face of the Christian faith Connie has embraced since childhood. Against a paralyzing sense of total betrayal, she must find her way with the help of the only God she has ever known, and be faithful to the vows she made on her wedding day, all without losing her husband or sight of herself.

The River Rolls On

The tabletop flat Mississippi Delta, and the lifestyle that geographic region provides, is both the setting and the backdrop for the story of a liberal lady activist. The explosive results of her efforts to bring racial and gender equality to a state where the fragrance of magnolia blossoms often masks the stench of good old' boy politics, are off the charts. When tradition battles change, everyone involved is somehow altered, willingly or not. This is the life-long lesson that June Bug McRainey truly learns only as death approaches, as she is forced to confront her life's actions and results, and decide if there is a need to make last-minute amends.

Blessings and Conflict

Victims of domestic violence and abuse are affected for life. This is a sad fact that Margaret Haywood embraced early on in the pages of **Hear My Cry**, **Paths of Judgment**, and **Lift up Mine Eyes**. As she fought her way out of the aftermath of the violence that marred and destroyed their entire family unit, she and each of her children, Brian, Sally and Jason, acted and reacted in drastically different ways. How have the scars of what each experienced affected and directed where each of these four people are today? In the pages of **Blessings and Conflict**, catch up with these captivating individuals that readers bonded with over thirteen years ago. See where each of them is today, and how the specter of violence has colored each of their lives.

Alive By Default

America's dynamic, but extremely polarizing First Lady is killed when the presidential aircraft she's aboard is blown out of the sky over the country's heartland. For White House correspondent Patti Hobgood, who missed the now ill-fated flight because of a bad batch of chicken salad, the queasiness in her gut is surmounted only by her suspicions of the official explanation of the tragedy. Patti's journalism background demands that she investigate, and when her journey circles through eastern European capitals and back to D.C.'s very back doorstep, the reporter soon learns why the First Lady is dead. And why she may get to question the deceased firsthand, unless she ceases all inquiry.

About the Author

John Shivers began writing for his hometown newspaper when he was only fourteen years old. As a lifelong wordsmith – some have called him a wordweaver – his byline has appeared in over forty Christian and secular publications, winning him seventeen professional awards.

Hear My Cry, his first novel, was published in 2005, and a dream of forty-four years was realized. **Three Gifts for Christmas** is John's thirteenth book, and the first Christmas themed book. Ten of those books are Christian fiction, two are mysteries, and one is a mainstream novel. Additional titles in all three genre are in the planning stage.

John and his wife, Elizabeth, along with Callum and Rosie, their irascible but much-loved four-legged children, live in his hometown of Calhoun, Georgia. They are members of the Plainville United Methodist Church, where John serves as the congregational Lay Leader. When their schedule permits, he loves to slip away to heaven on earth in the mountains of northeast Georgia, where he enjoys the music that his heart hears in those hills. He also finds deep inspiration in rural south central Mississippi, where his and Elizabeth's mutual roots are almost two hundred years planted, and where they have a second home get-away.

Made in the USA
Middletown, DE
22 December 2018